Victoria Marmot

and the

Meddling Goddess

Virginia McClain

Cover design by Natasha Snow

Works by Virginia McClain

The Victoria Marmot series:
Victoria Marmot and the Meddling Goddess
Victoria Marmot and the Inconvenient Prophecy
Victoria Marmot and the Shadow of Death
Victoria Marmot Book 4 is coming soon!

The Chronicles of Gensokai series:
Blade's Edge
Traitor's Hope

Short Stories
*Rain on a Summer's Afternoon**
*Note that you can get Rain on a Summer's Afternoon for free by subscribing to Virginia's newsletter

For Lee, for all the hours spent with the sapling.

VICTORIA MARMOT WAS unrolling her sleeping bag in a quiet mountain glade, the clearing surrounded by tall pines and a single oak with branches that gave it a shape rather like a hooded person carrying a scythe.

"Hello?"

She paused, as though unsure of where to find the best view of the star-filled night sky.

"Who is saying that?"

Her chestnut hair barely reflected the star light, her mint-green eyes flashing with confusion as her caramel skin darkened to the color of milk chocolate with her increasing ire.

"Who the fuck is hiding in the woods describing me like a damned dessert?"

She stared furiously into the woods, unable to ascertain the origin of the mysterious voice even as she reached for the knife on her belt.

"I will put a damned blade through the origin of the voice if it doesn't show itself RIGHT. FUCK-ING. NOW."

"Well, that seems uncalled for."

"Who said that?"

"I did," and, with a dramatic flourish few possess, a beautiful, milk-skinned redhead appeared in the forest before the young adventurer.

"Okay, crazy, naked nut job. Please stop narrating every damn thing that happens and go away."

"I can't. That's my job. I'm your narrator." With another flourish the graceful redhead produced a fabulous set of deerskin leathers and a flowing blouse to highlight her gorgeous figure.

"I don't need a narrator. Thank you for putting clothes on. And what the actual fuck is going on right now? Are you a hologram or something?"

"So tetchy! You do need a narrator. You're on an adventure."

"I'm on my weekly backpacking trip. I do this specifically to avoid people, especially people who refer to themselves in the third person, so please go back to whatever asylum you escaped from and leave me alone. I was about to enjoy some star gazing before falling into a blissfully exhausted sleep."

"You come out here every week to find a sense of normalcy after losing your parents in a freak boating accident six months ago, and don't pretend that you're ever exhausted enough to sleep properly since you lost your family."

Victoria's jaw hung open as she stared at the glorious redhead who seemed poised to turn all her carefully constructed escapism on its head.

"I know what my jaw is doing, you don't have to say it out loud! There's no one else to hear you. And how in seven hells do you know anything about me or my parents?"

"I told you, I'm your narrator. I'm supposed to be omniscient. I know everything about you, even things that you don't know about yourself."

"That doesn't make any sense. Why would I have a narrator? I'm not a character in a book. I'm a teenager *trying* to enjoy a nice little solo backpacking trip for the weekend. I do not need a psychotic hologram following me through the woods and analyzing me. I need to go to sleep. Preferably after catching the start of the meteor shower tonight."

"You *do* need a narrator because you are embarking on a great adventure."

"I'm backpacking on the side of freaking Mt. Humphreys. That is not a great adventure. It's a day hike that I'm drawing out as long as possible because I didn't have enough time to drive very far this weekend. Why on earth would this trip warrant a narrator, and seriously, even if you can answer that question, why the fuck would I believe that *you* are my narrator and not just some crazy woman who likes to wander the woods and freak out nature enthusiasts by popping up naked in front of them?"

Gwen carefully shaped her mouth into an attractive pout.

"I can see you doing it, I do NOT need you to tell me about it."

"I'm not saying it for you! I'm saying it for them."

"Who is THEM? There is no one else here, and if anyone were here, they would be able to see you too, so you don't need to narrate it. Unless you've brought a bunch of blind people here? Are there blind people hiding in this forest now too?"

Victoria threw a concerned glance at the woods that surrounded the small clearing where she'd unrolled her Therm-a-Rest and sleeping bag.

"Dude, seriously. Are you going to keep doing that? It is creeping me the fuck out!"

"Someone *has* to narrate this story. I can't just leave it unsaid, or they'll have no idea what's happening."

"They who— no, wait, you know what? Never mind. Fuck it. We're not getting anywhere that way. You said *someone* has to narrate this story. Does that someone have to be you?"

"I suppose not."

"Could that someone be me?"

"I suppose…. I *hate* first person narration. It seems like something only an angsty teen would do."

"Ok. Ms. Literati. Sorry to burst your critical bubble, but first person point of view is a perfectly valid form of narrative style, so you and your angsty teen comments can suck it."

"I'm only saying—"

"What were you going to do for the parts in my head?"

"What?"

"When it got to the parts where I think something important to the story, how were you going to narrate that?"

"Italics, I suppose. Why?"

"Just wondering if I could do the narration job with just my thoughts. You know, without saying everything I'm doing aloud, to avoid acting like an insane person."

"You keep throwing around those insane accusations. I'll have you know that's very offensive to sufferers of mental illness, who are often very productive members of society."

"Fine. You're right. I'm sorry. I know lots of people with mental health issues who are great, and decidedly not insane, but I don't know how else to describe someone who can't let go of an alternate reality that differs substantially from observable fact."

"*I* would call that a person stuck in a dimensional pocket, but that's neither here nor there."

"What? That's—never mind. Look, can I narrate in my head, or not?"

"Yes. I suppose that would work just fine."

"Fine. Then make me the narrator."

Gwen looked uncomfortable for a moment, as though that were a decision she didn't wish to make—

"Would you PLEASE stop—"

And then she did. Thank fuck. I no longer had to hear the delusional woman in front of me describe each of her own actions in detail.

"Thank you," I said. I wasn't sure if I was the one "narrating" now, but I didn't really care. I had just wanted her to cut that the fuck out. It was incredibly eerie to have someone describe your every move aloud, and it had been making it difficult to think.

"Ok…. So, can you go away now?" I asked, still unsure of whether or not I would even stay behind once this character left. I didn't know what a person with delusions like this was likely to do, and I didn't really feel like getting stabbed to death in my sleep. Despite what I'd acknowledged about lovely people with serious mental health problems—all true—I didn't know this woman at all, and a tiny percentage of people with mental health issues were truly unhinged and dangerous. The unhinged and dangerous ones likely just needed a better therapist and the right meds, but that wasn't going to make me any less dead if Gwen were one of them and found herself unable to resist the voices telling her to take my head as a trophy.

"Well, I'm afraid I haven't quite taken care of my role this evening," Gwen said, startling me out of my dark imaginings of her waving my bloody severed head in the wind. "I *was* your narrator, but I er… have another purpose too. Tonight, mainly, it's to get you started on your quest."

"My quest?"

"Yes, your quest." And with that statement, the leathers she was wearing somehow became a flowing gown that definitely brought forth Lady of the Lake style imagery, all flowing blue silks and shit. "The DM was supposed to show up for this, but he ran into a scheduling conflict, and since I was going to be here anyway, I offered to help out."

"The DM? Are you kidding me? Is this whole thing just an elaborate role playing game? I mean, honestly, that explains just about everything, including the sudden costume changes, but seriously, you need to let people know when they're going to be part of a LARPing event. Just showing up naked and calling yourself a narra—"

"No, no, The DM is just the name he goes by now, he's one of the original Fates, actually. Just likes to keep up with the times. Anyway, he can't make it tonight, so I suppose it doesn't really matter."

"The Fates? Seriously? You expect me to believe—" Gwen raised her voice and kept on going, as though I'd never interjected.

"And I'm SUPPOSED to tell you...."

She cleared her throat.

"Yes?"

"Are you finally listening?"

"Will it make you go away?"

"Yes."

"Then I'm listening."

"Your quest, Victoria Adelaide Marmot, is to find out what really happened to your parents."

And then, I shit you not, she literally disappeared. Yes. Literally. Not figuratively, and not as some asshats misuse literally to mean "very." She straight up evaporated into nothing. Where once she had stood was now empty space, and there was no trace of her in any direction. She hadn't even snapped her fingers.

So, thoroughly shitting my pants (figuratively of course), I packed up my overnight pack and booked it the hell back to my car. I was freaked out enough by her disappearing act to run away, but the thing that spooked me most was how much she had known about my weekend adventures and the real reason behind them.

She had been right on the money. I ran into the wilderness every weekend because it was the only place I could find a semblance of peace in a world that had snatched my parents away from me, over a year before I would graduate high school. And now, some lady who liked to stalk people in the woods and describe them like tasty snacks had shown up, known about my parents' deaths, and implied that they hadn't died the way I thought they did.

And that was more than I could fucking take, to-night.

CRAWLING INTO MY own bed, in the large, empty house my parents had willed to me, didn't made me feel any better. Part of me wished I hadn't allowed Gwen to scare me away from my campsite. Watching the meteor shower from the side of the mountain would have been spectacular, and probably worth the risk of getting stabbed to death by a delusional woman delivering quests, but I had been too agitated to think it through at the time. Returning to my newly acquired home had seemed the more reasonable option, even if it was depressingly devoid of other people. Pulling up to the darkened doorstep of my blue clapboard-covered home, in its quaint, gently-wooded Flagstaff neighborhood, hadn't made me feel any more secure than I had felt alone in the woods, and walking into the house was just one more reminder that I was alone in the world. Well, I suppose I had my great-uncle Algernon, but… that wasn't much comfort when he wasn't actually in town.

Getting ready for bed, my mind played the conversation I'd had with a total stranger in the woods on a endless loop. When my brain finally let me sleep, I was more agitated than I had been since my parents had failed to come home from their round-the-world journey.

I woke up so angry it was a physical sensation.

As I stared down my reflection, while brushing my teeth, I was practically vibrating with rage.

Who the fuck was this Gwen person anyway?

And I don't mean that in the figurative, "who does she think she is," type way, although, hey, that too while we're at it. But—who *was* she? She was the kind of nut job who went around claiming to be a narrator and a deliverer of quests, that's who she was. I should just ignore her and her ridiculous claims about my parents, but…

But she'd disappeared like she was straight out of Hogwarts. That could be some kind of special effect. It's not like I searched every inch of woods for her right after she ammscrayed from my line of sight, or like I could have searched well enough to eliminate the possibility that she'd used smoke, mirrors, and a hologram to fake her disappearance, even if I had tried to. She could totally be putting one over on me. It's not as though vanishing made the rest of what she said true. It was just that…

What she'd said about my parents…

Damn it!

I'd spent so much time trying to accept my parents' death. Every day since I'd gotten the call six months ago, it had been the main thing I'd been doing with myself. Gwen hadn't been wrong when she'd accused me of running into the wilderness to hide from people and…process things. It was what I was doing with every weekend backpacking trip, with every afternoon trail run I took into the mountains…

But I had researched my parents' death as fully as any seventeen year old could without retracing their every step. I had tracked down all of the records from their GPS, all of their emergency logs. Everything that their beacon broadcast the day that their boat was lost…. All of it.

It had taken me months to even accept that they were dead. That it wasn't all some ridiculous mistake. The possibility that they hadn't died that day…but was that even what the naked narrator lady was implying? That my parents were still alive? Or was she just suggesting that they hadn't died by drowning in the Indian Ocean?

I shook myself from where I'd gotten lost in the mirror and swore loudly when I checked the time on my phone.

Great. On top of everything else, I was going to be late for my first day at my new school.

~~~

I must have still been furious when I rushed into my first period physics class that morning. That's the only explanation I can come up with for why I decided to sass the teacher when she asked me why I was late. Well, that, or the fact that the bell had rung *while* I was walking through the door.

"Why are you tardy, Miss… Marmot? What a quaint name."

The teacher was a middle aged woman with lank black hair and what looked like a permanent sneer. I rushed past multiple rows of black-topped desks, each with pairs of stools supporting a variety of fellow teenagers, barely noticing any of the people around me, or the vaguely generic science paraphernalia around the room, and took a seat at the back. I replied while rummaging through my backpack for my notebook.
~~~

"Sorry. It's my first day. I got lost on the way here."

No. That wasn't the sassy part.

"And you believe that excuses your tardiness?"

I stared at her for a moment before replying.

"Well, it's kind of a one time excuse, so… yeah."

There we go! Sasstastic!

"Well, class, Ms. Marmot believes the rules don't apply to her. How does that make the rest of you feel?"

"We should punish her!" shouted an enthusiastic blonde kid from the front row.

Great. Next up, I expected someone to accuse me of turning them into a newt.

Before anyone could get my funeral pyre ready, though, the voice next to me spoke up.

"She smells amazing."

I turned, incredulous at the inanity of that statement, and found possibly the most handsome boy I'd ever seen staring at me with a disturbing look in his eye.

"What was that, Edik?" the teacher asked.

"Nothing, Ms. Rebuke. I said 'no hazing.' The school rules dictate that we shouldn't—"

I snickered and he stopped speaking. I hadn't meant to let the noise escape me, but… Rebuke?

"Do you find something funny, Ms. Marmot?"

Now the woman was suddenly standing right in front of my desk and I was too mesmerized by how quickly she'd moved to come up with a witty retort.

"No, Ms. Rebuke."

I barely managed not to chuckle saying her name. I felt bad though. Most people had no choice in their last names.

"If you are so intent on entertaining this class, Ms. Marmot, perhaps you can entertain us with today's lesson. The topic is dark matter. Please, why don't you enlighten us with your extensive knowledge on the subject."

Well, that was an odd punishment. I was a little surprised that dark matter was today's lesson, even though this was an AP physics class. It wasn't exactly an intro topic, but whatever, far be it from me to discourage interesting lesson plans. I shrugged.

"Ok. Do you want me at the front of the class? The chalkboard would be handy."

Ms. Rebuke said nothing, only glared at me.

I decided to stay in my seat.

"Dark matter is a popular theoretical explanation for all the excess mass in the universe," I began.

Did I mention that binge-watching Neil deGrasse Tyson's Cosmos remake was another way in which I dealt with my parents' death? Honestly binge-watching anything on Netflix should be considered an official stage of grief. Somewhere after denial and anger, but before acceptance.

"On its largest scale, the universe behaves in a way that suggests that there is far more mass in it than we can currently detect. The theory is that most of the universe's mass, therefore, is matter that we cannot see, sense, or detect with current instruments. Something like 99% of the universe is made up of this non-detectable mater, in fact—"

"That's enough Ms. Marmot! You may visit the principal's office at any time now. You certainly aren't needed here, as you've made it clear that you're already an expert on today's subject."

"Wait, are you kicking me out of—"

"Go!"

Ms. Rebuke sounded like she was ready to spit flames, so I didn't argue. I really hadn't meant to give her any grief to start with, but being marked tardy as I walked in while the bell was ringing, on my very first day at a new school, in a new town, when I had already woken up angry… I wasn't at my best. I had started to pack up my stuff when the stupidly handsome boy next to me spoke up again.

"I'll take her," he said, in the tone of someone who had been asked to help the less fortunate. "She won't know how to get there."

"Excellent, Edik. Please come right back."

I had a school map in my pocket, and the look in Edik's eyes still freaked me out a bit, so I headed for the door without looking to see if he was behind me.

UNFORTUNATELY, MR. DAZZLING Eyes was indeed with me as I walked out the door.

"You don't have to take me, really. I can find the office on my own."

As if I hadn't spoken, the dude wrapped his arm around my shoulder and started talking.

"Don't worry about Ms. Rebuke. She doesn't even teach physics, normally. She's the chemistry teacher. Just subbing, for some reason. Not sure where the real physics teacher is today, but have no fear, I won't allow her to harm you."

"Um…dude, can you take your arm off me, please?"

I like to ask before I force people to move in ways that are likely to hurt them.

"Oh, of course, my dear. How terribly forward of me! Wouldn't want to give anyone the wrong impression, would we? I'm awfully sorry. I simply… got caught up in you."

"That's weird, Eric."

"It's Edik, not Eric."

"Oh. Sorry."

I wasn't particularly sorry, because this guy was setting off my creep-o-meter something fierce, but I did like to get people's names right. I was in favor of people being addressed in whatever way they preferred to be addressed.

Edik though…. Not only was this guy's accent decidedly inappropriate for Arizona, but his manner of speaking was entirely wrong for this century. However, talking oddly wasn't a reason to bestow violence on anyone, and as he had removed his arm from my shoulders I decided he didn't require a knee to the balls just yet. Still, he was doing himself no favors with his "let me save you" talk and his lack of personal boundaries.

I spent the rest of our brief stroll through the featureless hallways trying to surreptitiously walk farther away from my escort, but he refused to give me more than a handsbreadth of personal space. Thankfully, a few well-marked turns down blandly lit hallways delivered me to an office that was leaking small, disturbing wisps of smoke from the crack where door met frame. Just as I was trying to tactfully tell Edik to hit the road, he saved me the trouble.

"I hate to leave you, my darling, but I cannot abide the smell of this place. Fare thee well!"

And before I could even thank Too Creepy To Be Handsome Anymore dude for unnecessarily guiding me to the door quite clearly labeled "Principal," he was gone.

"That… was decidedly weird," I muttered, before cautiously knocking on the door.

I am not overly versed in recreational drugs, but even I could tell it reeked of pot in this hallway, so I wasn't sure what I was expecting to see when the door opened.

A bushy-browed, grey-haired, long-bearded man in a crushed velvet bathrobe was definitely not on the list of things that crossed my mind in the few seconds' between when I knocked and when the door opened.

The giant wave of pot smoke that billowed around him was also a bit of a surprise. At least, in the sense that it was pooling out of an office clearly labeled "Principal" in the middle of a school day. It wasn't surprising given that wisps of smoke and pot reek had been pouring out of the office before the door even opened.

"Umm… is now a bad time?" I asked, unsure how to proceed.

"Is he gone?" the man asked.

"Is who gone?"

"That vampire twat, Edik."

"Umm… Edik left, yes."

"He hasn't got to you, has he?"

"What does that mean?"

"You're not in love with him, are you?"

"What?!"

"It's a long story."

The old man, who was speaking with a decidedly British accent, peered suspiciously down the hallway in each direction and then gestured me into the office.

I hesitated, if only because I didn't particularly want the contact high I was fairly certain would result from walking into that room.

"Come, come. If he's left, then now is the perfect time to talk."

"Ok."

I was a bit baffled. I hadn't even had a chance to explain what I was doing here.

"Ms. Rebuke sent me," I began, planning to confess my sassy sins, but the grey-haired man shut the door behind me and cut me off.

"I know, I know. Not sure what's got her knickers

in a bunch today. I suppose she's miserable about substituting for Physics again, but Ms. Squirrel is still unwell. Anyway, that hardly matters at this point. Come here, child, let me look at you."

Uh… weird. That was definitely a weird request. People I'd only just met asking to get a closer look at me was not something I was entirely comfortable with, but I wasn't getting any leering vibes from the old dude, so I let it slide. But then he was staring deeply into my eyes and tearing up, and that was a bit more than I could handle, creepy vibes or no. It was disturbing enough that I looked around the room. Anything to keep from locking eyes with the ones behind the half-moon spectacles in front of me.

The room was still smoky, but underneath the smoke it reminded me of an old cat lady's living room, minus the cats, plus a couple of very large lizards.

I was just about to ask about the origins of the six-foot-long iguana that lay along the back of a red velvet wingback chair, when my thoughts were completely derailed.

"You have your mother's eyes."

"What?!" I almost shouted, my eyes snapping back to the grey ones in front of me.

"Your mother, Tenzin, you have her eyes."

"You knew my mother?"

"Yes. Of course. Didn't you know?"

"Mister, I don't even know who you are!"

It was true. I assumed that this man was the principal of the school, but the pot smoke had made me doubt that a bit, and I certainly didn't know his name. I most assuredly had no inkling that he had known my mother.

"Didn't your parents tell you about me? Professor Bumblebee? I taught them both."

"What?"

I sat down in the red velvet wingback, despite the hissing of the iguana.

"Your parents both studied with me. Didn't they tell you? Surely you've wondered how they learned it all?"

"Learned what? My father was an English professor and my mother was a professional triathlete. I wasn't aware that they'd ever studied the same subjects."

My tone was probably bordering on insolence, but I couldn't help it. Between crazy ladies in the woods telling me that my parents hadn't died the way I thought they had and this guy revealing that he was an old family friend… I just didn't have enough energy left to stay polite.

"Well, let's see. Where to begin? What do you know exactly?"

"About what, Mr. Bumblebee?"

"Oh, call me Albert."

"Ok, Albert."

I would have asked why I was supposed to call my school principal by his first name, but a knock on the door stopped the words in my throat. I was so desperate to have a conversation that wasn't emotionally draining that I almost hoped it was Edik come to escort me to my next class.

It wasn't.

Albert opened his office door to reveal another student who looked about my age. He was slightly taller than me, and had long, black hair pulled into a ponytail to reveal high cheekbones, startling amber eyes, and skin the same shade as mine. For some reason, I couldn't take my eyes off of him.

"Mr. Topaz sent me to get the new student."

His voice was deep and quiet, and far more alluring than it should have been. I shook myself and turned to Mr. Bumblebee.

"Oh? Yes, yes. I suppose she should go to classes anyway." He turned his half-moon spectacles in my direction then. "Do come back, dear. We have much to discuss."

I nodded, numbly, and then stepped out the door and stood awkwardly next to the student who had come to retrieve me.

"Umm… hi," I muttered, lamely. What the hell. I was never tongue-tied in front of guys. "I'm Vic." I cleared my throat and proffered my hand.

"Seamus," he said, taking my hand and shaking it firmly before dropping it like it was hot.

If he had felt the same electric jolt up his arm that I had just felt up mine while shaking his hand, then I didn't blame him.

"Nice to meet you," I said, after an interminably long pause during which we said absolutely nothing but just stared at each other as if we'd never seen another human before.

"You smell good," he replied.

Right. Well, my day was officially stupid.

"**I**'M SORRY ABOUT that," Seamus mumbled.

"What?" I asked, no longer sure that we were both speaking English.

"Saying you smell good. That's creepy as hell. It's just… true."

I nodded. "Ok. As long as you acknowledge it's creepy and don't expect me to be flattered or anything…"

"Gods, no! I just… said it before I could think. I'm sorry. I've never said anything that weird before. I mean, not since I was like five."

"Right. Ok. You can stop apologizing now."

He nodded. I tried to take a deep, calming breath, and then realized that he smelled *amazing*. Like a pine forest and a mountain breeze and… gingerbread with chocolate sauce? What the hell!?

I shook myself and looked pointedly towards the hallway that I thought we should be walking down instead of standing awkwardly in front of Mr. Bumblebee's door.

Seamus finally caught on and gestured towards the hallway with one hand, while standing well back from me.

"Shall we?" he asked.

"Sure."

I gave him the same wide berth he'd given me. The man smelled better than anyone I'd ever met, and sent sparks shooting up my arm when we touched…. Did not need more of that right now.

~~~

"So, where are you from?" Seamus asked, as we wandered yet another bland institutional hallway lined with lockers. Honestly, this school was so drab it could have been any public high school in the US. How it managed to hide within its walls a cadre of teachers, seemingly all hailing from the UK, piloted by a oddball hot-boxing principal, was a mystery that would have fully enveloped my attention had I not been distracted by Seamus' attempts at conversation.

"What makes you think I'm not from here?" I
~~~

asked, before I could stop my typical knee-jerk response to the question.

"Well, you're new here, but you're a senior... I just assumed you moved here from somewhere else."

I took a deep breath and tried to remember that not everyone who saw my skin tone and eye shape assumed I was from a different country. It was hard, because I got that a lot.

"Sorry. I'm not having the best day. Colorado, I suppose."

"You're not sure?"

"Well, before Colorado we moved once or twice, and I spent most of my summers on a boat until recently."

"Well, that sounds interesting. Wanna talk about it?"

I chuckled. Seamus set me at ease for some reason, despite the annoying electric buzz I'd gotten when we first shook hands, and the weird smell comment. He didn't seem... demanding.

"I'd love to, but I suppose we should wait until after class."

I nodded towards the closed door that was labeled with the number that corresponded to the folded-over schedule I had wrestled out of my pocket on the walk here.

"Oh, yeah. Probably. Though I wonder some-times if he'd even notice if we all left the room…"

"Huh?"

"You'll see. Come on."

He pushed open the door and we shuffled in, just ahead of a handful of other students who had ar-rived from the opposite direction. I followed Sea-mus to a low table in the back of the room. The tables were set up in rows, with one aisle down the middle and three chairs per table. The room was drearily devoid of decoration save for a lone poster from the Dead Poets' Society.

It seemed as though our class wasn't full, as no one tried to sit with us and there was also plenty of room to spare at the other desks. I usually preferred to sit up front for my classes, but today apparently wasn't my day for it.

After class got started, I understood Seamus' seating choice perfectly.

The teacher, a balding man without a single memorable feature, started by reading some truly terrible poetry, and continued... by reading more of it. No one asked a single question and indeed, the man just paced the front of the room reading aloud from his book without even looking at a sin-gle student.

Despite my best efforts to pay attention, around the seventh poorly rhymed verse about a whale frolicking somewhere in Scotland I gave up.

Besides, Seamus' notes were too distracting. Mostly because they consisted of hilarious sketches about whatever oddity Topaz was describing in poem form.

A whale being harpooned, a royal carriage, a collapsed bridge… it was hard not to laugh aloud when he finally handed me a sketch of a blundering stick figure holding a goose.

This is truly terrible poetry, I wrote in reply. *Does he seriously do this every class?*

Seamus wrote back, *I think so. I mean, last year I only had him for a week as a sub, but this was all he did.*

I was amazed. Still, it wasn't long before we had abandoned the topic of Topaz's terrible poetry.

Is Vic short for Victoria? Seamus asked.

Yep. Not sure why my parents went full-on boring cat lady when they named me, but that's my legacy.

I watched Seamus smile while reading my reply, and swallowed hard. I was doing my best to think of him in purely friendly terms, but my body kept reacting to him in a really… emphatic way.

Not sure what my parents were thinking when they named me Seamus, TBH, he replied.

I raised an eyebrow at that.

I just assumed you were part Irish.

That was a lie. I hadn't assumed that at all. He didn't look even remotely Irish, but now that I thought about it seemed plausible enough.

Good guess. I am, actually. But I'm mostly Navajo, and I'm still bummed that I didn't get a much cooler name than Seamus.

Seamus sounds pretty cool to me.

Yeah, until you realize it's just Irish for James.

Huh. Do you have a nickname you prefer?

Nah. I just stick with Seamus. What about you? he asked.

At this point we weren't even pretending not to pass notes, we were just both hunkered over my notebook right in the middle of the table.

I already told you to call me Vic.

No, I mean heritage-wise. The Navajo is pretty obvious, but I just admitted to being part Irish. I was wondering what awesomeness produced those eyes…

I could feel blood rushing to my cheeks as I read the comment about my eyes. Part of me wanted to hurl at my own reaction. It was just a compliment, but, whatever, I was touchy about my eyes. Having someone appreciate them was… whatever. It made me blush.

Honestly, I don't know that my heritage does much to ex-plain my eye-color, but since you "admitted" to being Irish…

just Tibetan on my mom's side, and Dad's is more of a mystery. He never talked about his family much. If I had to guess, based on what he did say… Euro-Mutt and… African? Not the entire continent, obviously, but I seriously have no idea which country, or even which region, really.

Seamus had just started penning his reply when the door to the classroom flew open and slammed against the wall, loud enough to actually cause Mr. Topaz to pause in his reading.

Edik stood in the doorway, and I watched with growing dismay as his eyes scanned the tables until they reached the one where Seamus and I were sitting.

Before I could blink, Edik was standing in front of me and glaring at Seamus.

"What are you doing sitting next to *him*?"

"Um… listening to terrible poetry. What the seven hells are you doing here?"

I felt safe making the terrible poetry comment because as soon as Edik had left the doorway, Mr. Topaz had started up again without the slightest indication that he objected to Edik's batshit crazy entrance.

"Victoria, darling, you cannot possibly entertain this mongrel. He's absolutely beneath you."

"Edik. Seriously. What are you doing here? I'm in the middle of class."

"I came to tell you the truth. Your scent is so compelling that I cannot keep it to myself any longer."

I really didn't want to know where this was going. "Edik. You need to leave now. Keep whatever it is to yourself and just go, please."

"I cannot! I must tell you. It is a truth I cannot keep from you. We are meant to be. I am a creature of the night, and I love you.

I HAD NEVER been more relieved in my life to smell the earthy, cloying scent of marijuana than when Albert Bumblebee had wandered into Topaz's class for a "surprise audit."

Edik hadn't even said goodbye before glaring daggers at the principal and storming out.

As a bonus, Topaz had seemed reluctant to continue reading from what appeared to be a leatherbound journal of his own poetry after Bumblebee's arrival, and instead we had started a somewhat lively discussion of Twelfth Night, which had been part of the assigned summer reading.

Honestly, the rest of my day was pretty normal after that. At least until I got to swim practice.

Swimming was on the list of the few things in life that grounded me, much like backpacking, rock climbing, and trail running, so I had been looking forward to this first practice ever since I had woken up vibrating with anger.

My anticipation hadn't exactly diminished when I'd learned that Seamus was also on the swim team. Still, as I walked, dripping, from the showers in the locker room into the humid, chlorine-laden air of the pool, I was determined that even Seamus' mostly naked presence wouldn't distract me from getting into the zone.

That proved more difficult than expected.

He wasn't decidedly better looking than most guys who swim competitively, and I was *very* used to seeing guys who swim competitively wearing next to nothing. It was literally part of my everyday existence during swim season, and I had been swimming competitively since I was ten.

So, why, why, WHY could I feel Seamus' boy in the lane next to me as if it were radiating flames?

Luckily, swimming isn't the kind of sport that allows you to stop and ogle the swimmers nearby while you're in the water. But it shouldn't have been such a damned challenge to keep myself from trying to do just that.

I'd had crushes on guys on my team before, had even dated a teammate for a little while at my old school, but, usually, once I hit the water, nothing else mattered.

At least, on a normal day.

Today was clearly not a normal day.

As evidenced by the completely naked creep swimming right underneath me.

"WHAT THE ACTUAL FUCK!?!?" I screamed, pulling myself from the pool as though the water were lava.

Everyone was staring at me as I stood on the pool side shaking with rage, I could tell, but my eyes were fixed on the water, where Edik—still butt naked—was blithely hanging out near the bottom of the pool, without coming up for air, and waving gaily at me as though this were all terribly amusing and wouldn't we laugh about it later.

Before I could even draw breath to ask if anyone else saw what was happening, a giant ball of fur shot past my left arm and flew into the water, going straight for the nudist.

Suddenly the water was a giant froth of wolf, blood, and naked crazy person.

Despite what my brain tried to tell me about the low likelihood of a wolf diving into a school pool during swim practice, my eyes were quite convinced by the evidence to the contrary. I was too familiar with wolves to mistake it for anything else. The coat, the size, the lankiness, the flash of amber eyes that I saw briefly at one point when it came up for air… all of it shouted wolf. Especially the giant canines that were visible just before they tore into Edik's arm again.

Once the initial shock wore off, I took a quick look around and saw that the same shock was nowhere close to wearing off for my fellow swimmers. Indeed, many of them had already run for the changing rooms. Even Seamus was nowhere in sight.

Right. So this was going to be on me, then. Fine.

I had a moment of wanting to just let the wolf ravage the batshit weirdo who had been swimming naked underneath me, because, honestly… just… ew. But Edik probably didn't deserve to die for his crimes, and… well, I really didn't want the wolf to get killed. Although, since the wolf was attacking humans it was probably already sick, and there was no way it would be getting out of here alive if authorities of any type showed up. Besides, what the hell did I think I could do to stop a wolf from attacking someone, anyway? Other than lose an arm, that is.

Then a quiet voice spoke up beside me and I almost jumped out of my skin.

"Do you plan to just let them go on like that?" the voice asked.

I turned to see Mr. Topaz, of all people, standing

there still wearing the three-piece suit he'd donned for our class that morning.

"Um… did you have any ideas for getting them to stop?" I asked.

He shrugged.

"No. And it wouldn't bother me, normally, but I like that Seamus bloke and I wouldn't want him to get hurt. Edik's a git, anyway."

"What does Seamus have to do with any of this?"

I was beginning to wonder if Topaz was actually as batty as his poetry suggested.

"The wolf," he said, nodding at the churn of water ahead of us, "is your friend Seamus."

It might have been a bit early to deem Seamus a friend, but he seemed like a nice enough kid. He did not, however, seem like 130 pounds of canine fury.

"I am fairly certain that Seamus is *not* a timber wolf."

"Really? Interesting. Is he a mexican red or something? But he's all black… I'm not very good with animals."

This conversation was getting away from me fast. Just then, I heard a small scream and turned to see none other than Seamus, locked in Edik's unyielding grip. The wolf was nowhere in sight.

I wanted to ask what had happened to the wolf, or how Seamus had shown up without my noticing, or why he was suddenly naked, but I didn't take the time. I had been somewhat absorbed in talking to Topaz, anyway, so Seamus must have come running from the changing rooms just as the wolf ran off, and it all must have happened while I was staring in disbelief at my English teacher, who was suggesting that Seamus was somehow also a wolf. Giving up on figuring out how it had gone down, I went to split up what had now become a simple fist fight—well within my purview, and unlikely to lose me any extremities.

Not bothering to walk around the edge of the pool, I dove straight for the two young men entangled in the water, and as soon as I broke the surface on my way up, I also broke Edik's hold on Seamus' neck with the simple expedient of a punch to the face. Fun fact: getting punched in the face will distract most people who aren't used to it—and very few people are used to it. As soon as Edik loosened his grip, I grabbed Seamus by the shoulder and swam him towards the side of the pool. By the time Edik recovered, I had already thrown Seamus into a beached whale position on the side of the pool. I spun back to Edik, ready to receive whatever attack he might throw at me, my legs treading water and my hands in a fighting stance. I wasn't used to fighting in water (I would have to ask my sensei about incorporating that into an upcoming class though, it would be fun) but I was willing to bet that Edik wasn't used to it either, and by this stage I was looking forward to kicking his ass.

I was disappointed, though. As soon as Seamus was out of the water, Edik stopped trying to attack.

"Are you alright, my darling?" he asked.

I propelled myself towards the deck as quickly as I could.

"Get away from me, creep!" I shouted, while pulling myself out of the water as quickly as possible. Seamus was gone. That was weird as hell, since he'd seemed almost unconscious when I'd pulled him from the water and I'd only turned my back on him for a handful of seconds to see if Edik was going to keep fighting.

While my eyes tried, and failed, to locate Seamus, I felt a hand touch my ankle and kicked backwards, connecting solidly with what felt like Edik's nose. It gave a satisfying crunch and he gasped in pain, but I didn't turn back to see what he was doing. I just made a beeline for the ladies' locker rooms and hoped to hell he wouldn't follow me in there.

I WAS STILL shaking a bit when I stepped into the warm afternoon that awaited me outside of the pool building. I closed my eyes, letting the mountain sun heat my face up a bit before I started my walk home. With my eyes closed and the fall-scented mountain breeze in my lungs, I could almost pretend I was back home in Colorado. Almost. Opening my eyes always brought a tinge of disappointment as I took in a view that lacked a full range of white-capped Rocky Mountains. At least the view had *a* mountain. It could have been worse. It could have been the flatlands.

I still wasn't sure why my parents had kept a home in Northern Arizona that I'd never known about, or why they had left it to me only on the condition that I occupy it. It had required leaving the high school I'd been attending for the past three

years, and all the friends I'd made there, and starting over from scratch. When I'd first read the will
I'd thought that had been particularly cruel. High
school was hard enough without having to be the
new kid in your senior year… but then I realized
that my parents probably hadn't been planning on
dying. I suppose they hadn't really expected any of
this to come up just yet.

So the only odd thing, then, was that I hadn't
known about the place at all. I mean, isn't it a little
weird that they owned a whole house that I never
knew about? Also odd that they'd made a provision
in their will for me to occupy the house alone, even
if I was underage still. Technically, my great-uncle
Algernon was my legal guardian, but he was only
required to check on me once a month. We didn't
have to live together. My lawyers (yes, my inher-
itance had come with lawyers) told me that was
rare. But whatever, at least I had a place to live,
even if it was in a different state from everyone I'd
known for most of my life.

Still, after all the awkward silences, pitying looks,
and sympathy hugs I'd gotten after my parents had
died, moving twelve hours away from my friends
had seemed like a fine idea when the time came.
Not to mention how impossibly lonely our Colorado home had seemed after the accident.

I hadn't even made it a block away from the non-descript concrete building that was Flagstaff High School when I felt a hand on my shoulder, and Seamus wound up eating dirt.

I realized who it was halfway through the throw and did what I could to help him land well, but he still hit the ground with the kind of gasp that lets everyone know that it's going to take a minute to start breathing again.

"Shit. Sorry, Seamus. Don't do that."

Seamus still didn't have air in his lungs, so I just tried to help him to a standing position while he worked on re-inflating his lungs.

"My bad," he muttered, when he finally had a enough air to speak. "I should have known you'd be on edge."

I shrugged.

"Not a good idea to grab me when I can't see you, anyway. Muscle memory takes over."

He raised an eyebrow at that.

"I've been studying mixed martial arts since I was ten."

"Right. Ok. Mental note. Do not touch Vic without her explicit permission."

I nodded.

"Not a bad rule for all humans, really."

Seamus thought about that. He nodded, but then frowned.

"I'm pretty cuddly with my friends, though. Male or female, doesn't matter. I like to hug, and wrap my arm around people's shoulders and stuff."

I smiled.

"I'm not saying you shouldn't touch people, Seamus, just make sure they're cool with it first. You don't need a written waiver every damned time, but, you know, pay attention to body language and facial expressions, and if you're ever in doubt, just ask."

He still looked upset, so I continued.

"I, for one, love hugs from my friends. I just need to be able to see them coming. And if I ever don't feel like being touched, I sure as hell will let you know."

"Preferably before you knock the wind out of me," Seamus said.

I shrugged again.

"Preferably, but I make no guarantees. Don't sneak up on me. I've been trained to hurt people who do."

"Fair enough," he said. Then he hunched his shoulders and stepped back a bit. "Well, this makes half of my mission seem obsolete."

"Oh? What was your mission?"

"To thank you for saving my butt in there," he began, "and to offer to walk you home in case Pervy McPerverson decides to show up again."

That made me smile.

"I appreciate the gesture, Seamus, but I think I can handle Mr. McNoPants if I need to. After all, he's made it extremely easy for me to kick him in the nuts."

Seamus chortled briefly before looking serious again.

"I don't like the idea of you going home alone now that he's set his sights on you."

I was no longer smiling.

"Dude. Keep your overprotective alpha male shit to yourself. I can defend myself, and you have no responsibility to protect me. I'll see you tomorrow."

With that, I turned on my heel. I liked Seamus. He had a good sense of humor and he seemed like good company, but I had zero tolerance for patriarchal bullshit.

"Vic, wait! I didn't mean…"

I did not wait. At least he was smart enough not to try to make me stop walking away.

About a block later I caught a strange, dark form out of the corner of my eye, but when I turned to look at it, I saw nothing. My house was basically a straight shot down the road from where I stood, but

I decided to make a detour to see if whatever I'd glimpsed was following me.

Sure enough, after I turned right down a side street, I saw it again. This time I waited until I was sure the dark patch was in my peripheral vision and didn't break my stride, then suddenly flipped around and saw clearly what was following me.

A wolf.

And not just any wolf.

The same black wolf that had launched itself into the pool after Edik had shown up.

What. The. Fuck.

I stared at the wolf. It stared back. I considered my options.

It whined.

I ran.

RUNNING AWAY FROM a wolf is a stupid thing to do. It elicits a prey-chasing response in them and is not anywhere near the top of the list of things you should do if you *don't* want a wolf to chase you.

Which is why I was running towards the wolf.

It probably sounds stupid to you, but really, I was just trying to convince the wolf that I was the bigger, badder predator, and that it should run for the hills. Honestly, we were in the middle of Flagstaff, which, aside from not generally harboring wolves to begin with, was full of other humans, so the wolf should have been wary to begin with. Me charging him should have thoroughly convinced him that his jaunt into Humanville was over and he should head back to wherever he might have friends waiting.

Should have.

But didn't.

I stopped when I was only a few feet away from the creature, which was staring at me like I'd lost my mind.

I lowered my arms and coughed, as though that covered up the insane yelling I'd been doing up until a few seconds ago.

"Go away. There are humans here who would hurt you, especially after you attacked that guy in the pool."

Look, it's not like I thought talking to the wolf was going to work. But old habits die hard, and after my stint volunteering with the Colorado Wolf and Wildlife center, I was in the habit of talking to wolves. I didn't expect him to listen to me. I'd spent a year's worth of weekends and vacations working with wolves who had always seemed like they were listening, but then went ahead and did whatever it was they had planned to do to begin with. Which, to be honest, I attribute to wolves just not giving a fuck, rather than wolves not understanding human speech, but however you slice it, wolves don't just take advice from humans and do what they say.

"Go on, bud. I know it's interesting here with all the weird smells and free food and stuff, but it's not safe and… and ok, you're really starting to creep me out with that."

That last part was in response to the wolf looking for all the world like he was chuckling when I said the words free food.

"Please go away," I tried again.

Then the wolf stretched a bit, nodded once, and walked away.

THAT NIGHT I was exhausted. Pants-shittingly eerie wolves aside, it had been a weird day, no matter how you cut it.

I had been ready to collapse into bed as soon as I got home, especially after the night I'd had previously, full of crazy narrators and bomb drops about my parents' deaths, but I decided to be a responsible not-quite-adult and microwave myself some leftover Chinese food before showering and collapsing into bed with a good book.

Luckily, none of my classes had assigned much in the way of homework, seemingly wanting to ease students into the transition from summer. I'd have to give an oral account of everything I'd done over summer vacation in Spanish tomorrow, but since I'd grown up speaking Spanish with my father anyway, I didn't feel the need to prepare.

I wasn't sure what time it was when I finally drifted off to sleep, several chapters into the latest Twenty-Sided Sorcerer book, but I was disconcerted to find the lights turned out when I woke up a few hours later. I didn't remember turning them off. Nor did I remember leaving the window open, but the breeze that caressed my face definitely brought with it the smell of pine needles and fresh earth, and those were not smells that originated inside my air conditioning unit.

I casually reached for my bedside lamp with one hand, all the while sliding my other hand under the pillow to grasp for the cell phone I vaguely recalled shoving under there after spending more time than I'd actually wanted to checking Facebook before starting to read.

At the same moment my left hand turned on the bedside light, my right hand connected with my cell phone.

The light blinded me briefly, even though I'd closed my eyes as it came on, but soon I was able to see a dark figure standing on the far side of the room.

"Step any closer, and I'll call the cops," I said, brandishing my cell phone. Of course, I'd already hit my speed dial for police dispatch, but whoever the fuck was standing inside of my room didn't need to know that just yet.

"I'm sorry, Victoria," said a vaguely familiar voice, as the figure stepped out of the shadows. "I didn't mean to startle you."

My jaw dropped as Edik stepped into the light of the lamp.

"What in the name of ten kinds of hell are you doing in MY BEDROOM?!" I shouted.

The small, closed-mouth smile that had been gracing Edik's lips fell, and his eyebrows raised in confusion.

"I just came to watch you sleep," he said.

"What the fuck do you mean, you came to watch me sleep?! That's the creepiest godsdamned thing I've ever heard. GET OUT OF MY HOUSE, YOU FUCKING PERV!"

Edik looked as though I had slapped him, but I wasn't about to be deterred.

"Seriously, get out of my house before the cops get here," I said, as he took a step closer.

"You called the cops?" he asked, looking for all the world like a stricken puppy.

"Yes, I called the cops. THERE'S A STRANGE MAN IN MY BEDROOM."

I have to admit I was partially yelling to make sure that whoever was listening over dispatch heard what I was saying. I had to hope that the GPS chip in the phone would give them my location.

"But it's just me. Surely you don't need them to come now?"

"Edik, did I say or do anything today that made you think I wanted you to visit me at all, let alone IN MY BEDROOM?"

"No, not exactly but… but can't you feel it, Victoria? Don't you feel the connection between us?"

"No, Edik. I do not. I feel no connection. All I know is that you're a very attractive, but probably sociopathic, classmate who has shown up uninvited not only to my HOUSE, but to my freaking BED-ROOM, after, let's not forget, showing up to my swim practice butt naked and swimming underneath me like some kind of psychotic seal. Now, I'm going to ask you one more time to GET THE FUCK OUT OF MY HOUSE."

I was beginning to feel that Edik might be a little bit slow, as he persisted in not walking away from me, even though I could hear sirens in the distance already.

"But you're supposed to be the one who understands me, the one who is finally able to love me despite my being… being a… m-m-monster."

The way his lips pouted as he said that last part really made me want to hit him. So far he seemed like he WAS a fucking monster. After all, what the hell else do you call someone who breaks into your house at night to watch you sleep and then doesn't leave even after you call the cops?

"Get. Out. OF. MY. HOUSE!"

Instead of doing as I asked, the asshole insisted on stepping even closer to the bed, and I finally decided to stand up and back away, lest he try to pin me down.

This appeared to have been a mistake, as he covered the distance between us so fast that I couldn't even track it, and then pinned me to the wall. His body pressed against mine, and his arms pushed my shoulders back. At least I was standing upright.

"Do you have any idea how your smell drives me to distraction?" he asked, face buried in my hair, winning the award for creepiest shit ever said to me in my entire life.

"No, and you have one more second to back away from me before I will be forced to kick your ass," I said, with more confidence than I actually felt. Edik was a good six inches taller than I was, and had at least fifty pounds on me if I was any judge of muscle mass, but I was banking that he'd never been taught how to fight, especially after how quickly he'd backed down at the pool earlier.

"Victoria, I—"

His second was up. I'd really only given it to him to gather my own courage, not because he deserved any sort of second chance.

I stepped hard on his instep and buckled his arms at the elbow with simultaneous strikes from my forearms, then reached forward to grab the back of his head and pull his nose down to meet my forehead. Even as I did this, my knee came up and rammed into his crotch as hard as it could.

Edik collapsed into a pile on the floor just as I'd hoped, but I felt like I'd head-butted a tree, and slowly braced myself against the wall to hold the dizziness at bay.

Just as I sank to the floor with my back to the wall, I heard a rush of footfalls coming up the stairs. Without any announcement, the door burst open and a bunch of armed officers in uniform flowed through with their guns raised. I'd never been happier to see a cop, or seven.

I was just working on staggering back to my feet when one of the officers crouched down in front of me.

"Are you alright, miss?" she asked.

The voice caused a faint tremor of recognition to pass through me. I looked into the woman's face and tried to focus my blurring eyes for a moment. Focusing hurt, but through the pain I had a moment of full recognition, just before my vision started to darken.

"What are you doing here?" I asked the wild-haired redhead in uniform.

"Shh…" she said, holding a finger to my mouth, as blackness overtook me.

"Damn it, Gwen," I muttered, slumping to the floor as consciousness fled.

I'D WANTED TO ask Gwen a number of questions, but, of course, she was gone as soon as I came to.

It took a while for the rest of the cops and EMTs to leave, but luckily they were willing to take my statement in my own kitchen instead of making me go to the local precinct. I'd had a much harder time convincing the EMTs not to drag me to the hospital, but I downplayed the head-butt to Edik's brick-like skull and played up shock as the reason for my fainting. It wasn't that I wanted to ignore a concussion, it was just that I couldn't handle the thought of spending the night in a hospital alone.

The cops asked who they could call for me, but the only family I had nearby was my great-uncle Algernon, who was 85 and probably didn't need the hassle of being woken up by the cops at 2AM, so I said no one.

When everyone had filed out, I heaved a sigh of relief and turned to head up to my bedroom. I desperately needed to get some sleep. But just as I turned towards the staircase, I heard a scratching noise on my front door.

"What the…"

I wandered to the door and looked out the peephole. I couldn't see anything, but the scratching redoubled, coupled with a light whining sound.

I reached for the lock, then thought better of it. I turned around, went to the nearest closet, grabbed my field hockey stick, and THEN went to turn the lock on the door, field hockey stick brandished threateningly all the while.

My open door revealed none other than the wolf who had been following me home earlier.

"What are you doing here?"

It was a sign of how exhausted I was that I was talking to the wolf instead of panicking about having a large predator on my doorstep.

It whined again, and nudged its head towards the door, as though asking to come in.

"No. Dude. I need to sleep. Whatever wolfy business you think you have with me is gonna have to wait."

The whining increased, and the wolf stared at me resolutely.

"Seriously, I just need to get some slee—"

I didn't finish my thoughts on getting a full eight hours of rest, because at that moment both the wolf and I turned to look up the stairs, where we'd just heard a ridiculously ominous bump from my bedroom floor.

"**Y**OU'VE GOT TO be fucking kidding me," I mumbled, even as the wolf let forth a low growl that made my skin crawl. I glanced at him, just to be sure that the growl wasn't directed at me, but sure enough, he was staring at the ceiling.

"Well, should we head upstairs and see what's making all that racket?" I asked, even as I moved towards the staircase.

I was experiencing a weird mixture of fear and anger. Honestly, if I hadn't been so pissed off at the idea of Edik breaking into my bedroom *again,* especially after he'd just been carted off by the cops, I think I would have been cowering in a corner. As it was, I was ready to tear someone's fucking head off. Or at least laugh maniacally while I watched the wolf do it.

I took a deep breath as I neared the top of the stairs. If I was too worked up, I might incite the wolf to violence before it was strictly necessary. Although, I was having a more and more difficult time believing that the response to Edik shouldn't just be an immediate grab for the jugular.

Maybe one more calming breath before I opened the door…

The wolf was right on my heels, his head pushed up against my hip, as he tried to wrangle positioning so that he would enter the room first.

"Hey, there, Fang," I whispered. "No need to go all overprotective male on me. I can handle this. You're just here in case I knock myself out head-butting this asshole a second time."

The wolf growled, but took a step back.

"Look, if the nut shot works as well as it did before, you can pee on him while he's down."

The snarl that followed looked like it was supposed to be an imitation of a smirk. I shook my head. *Wolves do not emulate human facial expressions,* I reminded myself.

One more deep breath, and…

I pulled the door open and then instantly bent down to grab the wolf by the neck as he attempted to lunge past me, a deep-throated growl on his lips.

"Hold up!" I shouted to the enraged wolf that I had no business trying to restrain. Luckily, he decided not to turn his ire on me and continued to growl at the figure that sat in the middle of my floor.

"That," I said, standing up, but keeping one hand nestled in the fur of the wolf's neck, "is not Creepy McStalkerpants."

"**G**WEN?" I ASKED, unsure where to start. "What the fuck are you doing here? And why didn't you stick around earlier, if you were just going to show up again?"

"If you don't want me around, I can leave." Gwen stood up as she spoke, wiping imaginary dust from her spotless leather leggings.

"I didn't say that. But you know… you could have come and knocked on the door or something, instead of appearing here in my bedroom. Or even… I don't know, called me, like a normal human being."

"Phones are a hassle, you were busy with the cops and I didn't want to disturb you, and… I dropped something up here earlier."

That sounded like a blatant lie.

"Right…" suddenly I was glad that the wolf was here with me, even though it should have scared the crap out of me. I kept my field hockey stick raised. Just in case.

"I was just looking for the light switch when I ran into the end of your massive bed."

"Oh?" I guess that explained why she'd been on the floor when we'd come in.

"Why do you have a king sized bed, anyway?"

"Because I like to spread out when I sleep. Why do you care?"

"Because I like to move stealthily and the damned thing knocked me on my ass."

"I don't see how that's the bed's fault."

"You wouldn't."

"Mind telling me why you're here?"

Gwen just leveled her emerald eyes at me and stared until I blinked.

"I have a message for you."

"Ok…"

She flipped her fiery hair over her shoulder and looked pointedly at the wolf.

"Just you."

"Seriously? He's a wolf. Who's he going to tell? And besides, I don't really trust you at the moment, so I'd rather he stayed, thanks."

It might be insane to trust a wild animal I'd just

met more than another human, but I'd had a bad streak with humans lately, and I'd never had a wild animal do anything I wouldn't expect it to do. Well, ok, yes, except this guy following me and seeming like he was listening to me, but you get what I'm saying.

"Fine, he can stay, but I'm still casting a silencing spell on the room."

"A what?"

"A silencing spell."

"Am I supposed to know what that is?"

"I think the name is pretty self-explanatory."

"Yes, but the name implies… you know… magic."

"What tipped it off? The word spell?"

"Yeah, but… since magic isn't real, I assume you'll explain what you're *actually* going to do."

"Who said magic isn't real?"

"Um… everyone? For like the last 200 years or so?"

"Tsk, tsk, little girl, didn't your parents teach you *anything*?"

I didn't bother to reply, simply because I wasn't used to arguing with crazy people. If Gwen wanted to believe there was magic, how on earth was I going to argue with her? It's like when someone says that you can't prove to them that there aren't teeny, tiny, weightless, invisible unicorns who become insubstantial whenever you try to touch them dancing on your head right now. You can't disprove that kind of thing, you just know better.

Gwen gestured around the room for a bit, and then her eyes glowed a bright green for a few seconds. That weirded me out, but I wasn't sold on the idea that it was magic. You could buy all kinds of fancy contacts these days. I knew a girl who would put white contacts in her eyes and go sit in a park for hours at night, just to freak out the neighborhood kids. Folks need their hobbies.

"So, did you set up our cone of silence?"

"This is *not* an episode of Get Smart."

"You sure? It kinda feels like one."

Gwen just glared at me again. I felt that was an unfair number of malevolent eye gestures in my direction, when she was the one who had abandoned me after I'd been attacked AND the one who had broken into my house afterwards, making me think that my stalker was back.

I tried to return the glare, but wound up merely squinting. I probably looked like I had gas.

"Wanna tell me why you're here, now?" I said, when I'd given up on the staring contest.

"Are you sure you're ready? Would you like to sit down first?" she asked.

"Gwen, for fuck's sake, just tell me!"

"Tomorrow the triangle will be complete!"

I WOULD LOVE to tell you what the hell Gwen meant by that, but she poofed out of existence right after she'd made that announcement. Literally. There was an actual poofing sound.

I stared at the wolf and slowly slid my way down the wall next to my bedroom door.

"What the fuck is going on with my life?" I looked around at the Princess Bride, Harry Potter, Moana, and Doctor Who posters that covered my walls, but they seemed disinclined to help.

The wolf whined a bit, and tucked its head under the hand that wasn't holding the field hockey stick.

"I have psychos creeping into my bedroom at night, crazy women who can poof in and out of existence showing up to relate cryptic messages…" I hesitated and looked down at the large, amber-eyed wolf currently resting its muzzle peacefully on my leg. "And a giant, friendly wolf that followed me home."

The wolf whined a bit.

"I feel like I'm losing my damned mind."

I looked around my bedroom and realized that I wasn't going to be able to fall asleep here. I was exhausted, but the thought that Edik might come back, or that Gwen would poof in whenever she felt like it… a shiver crawled along my spine and I stood up.

"Come on, wolf. I can't sleep here and you… probably need to get back to wherever your pack is."

To my astonishment, the wolf got up and followed me without complaint.

Until we got to the front door, where it resolutely sat down and refused to cross the threshold.

"Come on, buddy. I can't keep a wild wolf. It's illegal, and you'd hate it. I don't have anywhere close to the acreage you'd need to be comfortable. Surely you have a pack somewhere."

The wolf didn't respond with any sort of noise or gesture, but it remained resolutely in place.

"Right. I'm still talking to a wild animal. Thanks for reminding me that I'm going cuckoopants."

The wolf snorted, far too close to a human chortle for my liking, and then headed for my living room.

"Seriously?" I sighed, shutting the door and locking it, not wanting to let anyone else show up uninvited in my house tonight if I could help it.

I stepped into the living room, just in time to see the wolf disappear on the other side of my couch.

A heartbeat later, Seamus was standing on the far side of the couch, naked, or at least, I was pretty sure he was naked. If he was wearing pants they were… incredibly low.

I swallowed and tried not to scream.

"Do I have a sign painted on me somewhere saying 'please surprise me naked'?"

"Vic, I'm really sorry. My clothes are outside. I can run and get them, but I wanted to show you the truth first."

"The what?" I asked, my foggy brain finally realizing that I couldn't see the wolf anymore.

"The truth. You kept talking about losing your mind and I thought… shit, maybe this wasn't a good idea."

It was taking a lot of effort not to launch myself at Seamus with the field hockey stick, and maybe he could tell that I was struggling, because his face looked pretty concerned all of a sudden.

"You have 30 seconds to explain yourself well enough to keep me from applying this stick to your head."

"Fine. Right. Ok. Look, I'm not supposed to talk about this, but… you're clearly not a non, and… Gwen did magic in front of you, right? So, I shouldn't get in trouble, but… damn it, I've never had to explain this to anyone else before!"

"Start making sense quickly, Seamus, you have 15 seconds." I adjusted my grip on the field hockey stick and settled into a fighting stance.

"I'm a werewolf."

"What?" I almost dropped the field hockey stick.

"I'm not naked because I want to sex you up or anything, and I'm not stalking you, I just… I followed you because I was worried that Edik would try another stupid stunt like the one he pulled at the pool, but you made it clear you didn't want me around, so I tried to just stay nearby and hope I would hear it if you needed help. I must have fallen asleep, because I didn't hear anything until the sirens were most of the way here. I tried to get in, but your doors were all locked, and by the time I'd decided to try breaking a window or something, the cops were already here. Then it seemed like they took care of Edik somehow, because he was out cold and in handcuffs when they dragged him out of here. I waited for them to leave in order to check on you. But then, well you know the rest of it, we heard that thump upstairs and now… well, crap.

You seem so… exhausted? Upset? Alone? I don't know, I didn't want to leave you alone, but I was worried you'd try to call animal services on me or something, so I decided the best thing was just to tell you the truth. I mean, you saw Gwen do magic, Edik straight up told you he was a creature of the night, and you smell like one of us, so I figured… crap. You think I'm insane, don't you? Look."

And then suddenly I was staring at the wolf again. He was just standing there, amber eyes and wolfy ears pointed right at me.

"See."

Now I was looking at Seamus again. Right where the wolf had been.

That was about the time my legs gave out.

OK. FINE. WEREWOLVES existed. By the time Seamus had left last night, there really hadn't been any arguing that. I did briefly try to convince myself that it was a truly elaborate prank, but in the end I couldn't figure out how it worked if it was, and, oddly enough, Occam's razor suggested that Seamus actually turning into a werewolf really was the more likely explanation. In the end, the fact that I could run my fingers through the wolf's fur and then be sitting next to a naked Seamus half a second later—and it was a sign of how stunned I was by the whole revelation that sitting next to a naked Seamus didn't phase me at all—well, what other explanation was there?

Of course, the best "scientific" explanation I could come up with was that Seamus was somehow pulling a wolf through an inter-dimensional pocket and trading consciousnesses with it, but that sounded almost as far-fetched as the idea that the whole thing was magic, so I kept it to myself.

Meanwhile, after eventually coming to terms—at least marginally—with the idea that Seamus was actually able to turn into a wolf at will, I kicked him out so that I could finally get some sleep.

Then I'd remembered that the thought of sleeping in my own bed made my stomach turn, and I'd set up camp on the couch. It wasn't rational that I felt in any way safer there, but my brain wasn't looking for reason, it was just looking to not go upstairs and be reminded that some psychotic asshat had shown up in my room in the middle of the night.

Despite how exhausted I'd been, sleep was a struggle. My brain kept turning over the things that Seamus had said. He was a werewolf, and I was… he wasn't sure, but he knew I was something, probably a were, just not a wolf.

All of which was preposterous. Werewolves were one thing… maybe. Me turning furry at will? Well, that was insane. I'd know if I had an animal form I could call on whenever I wanted. The idea that I'd somehow missed my ability to turn into something with four legs whenever I felt like it was just stupid.

And whenever I'd managed to stop thinking about the ridiculousness of a world where a guy from my english class could turn into a wolf, I'd gone right back to thinking about some douchetart showing up in my bedroom while I slept.

Sometime after the sun started to rise, I drifted off to sleep.

And was woken by my alarm almost immediately afterward.

"Fuck everything," I muttered, rubbing my eyes and hating life.

I debated just skipping school. After all, I would be useless after the negligible amount of sleep I'd gotten… but even as I thought about slinking upstairs and curling up in my bed, my stomach twisted. Memories of head butting Edik came flooding back, and I realized that I wasn't likely to get any more sleep, even if I stayed home.

"I repeat. Fuck everything."

I took a quick shower, scarfed a bowl of cereal, and trudged off to school as quickly as my sluggish legs would allow.

~~~

"I'm actually a vampire."

"What?!" I was trying to whisper, but I was so
~~~

flustered that freaking Stalky McStalkerson was still my lab partner, despite the fact that he had been taken away in handcuffs the night before, that I was raising my voice more than I'd intended.

He was supposed to have spent the night in prison and not been allowed to attend school today. The cops had told me we were supposed to have a court date on Thursday to establish a restraining order. I wasn't supposed to have to see him until then. But my lawyers (yes, I have lawyers, my parents left me a whole estate, there was a lot of paperwork involved) had called me this morning while I was walking to school to inform me that, despite everything I had told them and what the police had confirmed with them the night before, Edik had been released immediately. In addition, none of the law enforcement officials who had dealt with him seemed to recall any sort of violation of my rights. My lawyers were baffled and looking into it.

In the meantime, Sir Creepsalot was sitting right next to me in class with a face that didn't look at all like I had head-butted him the night before.

I felt like I was losing my mind.

Which may explain why I wasn't all that surprised by the words coming out of his mouth.

"I'm a vampire."

I simply stared at him. He was clearly not in the best place mentally. After all, who thinks it's ok to break into someone's house and watch them while they sleep? I tried not to think about how fucked up the night before was, and took a deep breath.

"And why, exactly, do you think you're a vampire?" I asked. I glanced at the front of the room to see if Ms. Rebuke was getting ready to send us both to the principal, but she seemed distracted by some disgusting blob that one of the students had created over one of the Bunsen burners. I wasn't clear why they were using the Bunsen burners in physics class, but I had bigger problems to worry about at the moment.

"I don't *think* I'm one. It's just what I am. It's why I'm different. It's why no one understands me."

My eyebrows lifted towards my hairline and I had a hard time keeping my face from reading as "you're batshit nuts!" when I turned to look at Edik.

"Um… have you considered that no one understands you because it's socially and morally unacceptable to show up in people's bedrooms and watch them sleep without an invitation?"

"No. That's not it. I'm a vampire. I drink human blood. Humans can tell I'm a predator and I make them uncomfortable. But you're different."

"No, I'm not. You *definitely* make me uncomfortable."

"It's not that. It's your smell. You smell different. And I can't tell what you're thinking."

"I have a good poker face and I don't wear gaudy perfume. That doesn't mean anything mystical. It means you should give me my space."

"No. You're special. I can tell. Here, look."

Some form of sheer morbid curiosity had me turn to look at Edik. What I saw was not reassuring. The way that Edik's teeth caught the sun was entirely disconcerting, and it fully explained why I'd never seen him smile with his mouth open up till now.

"You had your teeth encrusted with diamonds? Doesn't that cut your mouth up all the time?" I asked, trying to keep the pitch and meter of my voice level, despite wanting to scream across the room that I was paired up with a lunatic.

"I didn't *have* my teeth encrusted. They *are* diamonds. My whole skull is made of diamond. It's part of who I am."

This was going a bit far for an emo fantasy, or strange divergent cosplay, or whatever the fuck this was. It was too much. Ok, fine, his teeth were sparkly. Disconcertingly sparkly. And he was disturbingly handsome as well. But whatever the explanation was: "I'm a vampire," or "I'm a crazy person who shouldn't be allowed to be in school with the people I stalk," it amounted to the same thing: I was soooo done talking to him.

"Edik, I hate to say this—no, scratch that, I don't hate to say it, I just don't want you to attack me again, but I'm going to say it anyway—I don't believe that you're a vampire. And even if you are, you really need to stop talking to me. I'm working on filing a restraining order against you. I can't believe the cops let you come to school today."

I was agitated beyond tact and well into honesty. I didn't have the emotional fortitude to protect this guy's feelings, and frankly, he didn't deserve to have his feelings protected. I don't have much patience for guys who break into my bedroom and then corner me. Go ahead, accuse me of overreacting.

"The cops can't stop me. I just altered their memories. Same as I'll have to do with the girls who just noticed me showing you my teeth. But that's ok. They're just humans."

"I'm not sure which part of that I find most disturbing, so I'm not going to analyze it much. But seriously. You need to leave me alone. I want nothing to do with you, vampire or human."

"Vampire."

"Ok. Fine. Go away, vampire."

"We're lab partners."

"We're lab partners who are about to try to get each other arrested."

"I wouldn't have you arrested."

"Fine. I'm a lab partner who is going to get you arrested. Either way. Stop. Talking. To. Me."

"But, Vic—"

"Do you need me to knee you in the balls again?"

Edik's mouth slammed shut, and I wondered how he reconciled the idea of being a vampire with the simple fact that he got pwned by me last night. Not that I wasn't a very competent fighter, I was, but still. Vampires in all the books I'd read were supposed to be hot shit when it came to physical defenses. What kind of vampire gets taken down with a nut shot from a normal human that he outweighs by 50lbs?

~~~

It wasn't my first time being the new kid in school, so I was accustomed to the attention that one generally garners just by dint of being an oddity. Of course, I was usually considered odd enough that I continued to garner a bit of extra attention even after the initial new girl obsession had worn off. But
~~~

just because I was used to the attention didn't mean that I liked it. It wasn't that I couldn't stand being the center of attention; class presentations and theater performances didn't bother me. It was more that I hated the kind of attention that being the new kid garnered. It was rather like what I assumed it felt like to be in a circus sideshow. The looks were long and leering, filled with a derogatory curiosity that left you feeling like you needed a shower.

Imagine my delight then, when, during my second period class, whilst I blearily settled myself into a seat at the back, I noticed a student I hadn't seen yesterday. More than one person was looking straight at her and whispering in a way that clearly told me she was either new, or a pariah of some kind. Either way, she was taking the spotlight off of me. She sat calmly in the row directly ahead of me, and her dark, tightly-curled hair, pulled into a thick braid down her back, was all I could see. I smiled to myself at the idea of someone else getting stared at for a while, and then instantly regretted it.

"Ms. Marmot! What are you so smug about this morning? Is there something you would like to share with the class?"

What was Rebuke even doing in this class? I'd just escaped first period physics with her and was supposed to be in English with Topaz. She must be subbing again. I sighed.

"No, Ms. Rebuke, I was just smiling after relieving myself of some painful gas buildup. Thank you for asking though."

Oh dear. Filters were down after a night of almost zero sleep and a morning full of stalker. Perhaps she would be distracted by my self-deprecating humor? A chorus of laughter sounded around the classroom, but one look at her revealed that my joke had done little to deflect her ire.

"Ms. Marmot, are you under the impression that you are funny?"

"Everyone farts, Ms. Rebuke. I believe there was a book about it."

I bit my own tongue after that slipped out. *What the hell is wrong with me?* I didn't usually talk back to teachers, no matter what they said to me. Although, to be fair, I'd never had a teacher dislike me quite as strongly as Ms. Rebuke seemed to. It must have been the cumulation of stress and exhaustion over the past few days, but I couldn't seem to keep my mouth shut.

"Ms. Marmot! Do you *wish* to visit the principals' office again?"

"Actually, yes. I have a number of questions for him." I startled even myself with that one.

It was small consolation that the new kid at the table in front of me seemed to find my little display amusing, as I watched Ms. Rebuke's face take on a deep shade of vermillion. While my brain tried to regain control of my tongue, I drowsily wondered what she would do next. Since I'd just asked to be sent to the principal's office, the threat of sending me there lost much of its weight. On the other hand, allowing me to remain in the classroom would undermine her authority.

I briefly regretted having challenged the woman's authority, until I remembered that I'd never actually done anything to set her off except answer her questions on the first day of class, when she had seemed to hate me instantly for no reason. I wasn't proud of undermining her authority in her own classroom, but I was happy to demonstrate to her that it wasn't a good idea to go around being horrible to people for no reason.

"GO. TO. MR. BUMBLEBEE'S. OFFICE. IM-MEDIATELY!"

Her face was so red by the time she spoke that I was surprised not to see steam exuding from her ears like a Warner Bros cartoon. I stood up and shouldered my backpack.

Just as I reached the front of the room and turned towards the door, I heard a voice mutter, "Incidi!" and felt something sting my shoulder. I turned to find the new kid pinning Ms. Rebuke's arms to her sides and… snarling?

I inspected my shoulder, but found nothing wrong with it. The young woman, who looked like a younger version of Zoe from *Firefly*, left Rebuke where she was and came to usher me out the door and take a look at my shoulder.

"Looks like she missed," she said, once we were on the other side of the classroom door.

"Um… I felt something hit my shoulder, but… well, I feel fine otherwise."

I was struggling to string a sentence together. This girl was gorgeous, and everywhere she touched me felt like my skin was on fire. I'd never found a woman attractive before, but my body didn't seem to give a damn about that small detail.

"So she *did* hit you? Why aren't you cut, then?"

"I'm not sure. What did she throw at me?" I asked.

The young woman's eyebrows raised in confusion. For a moment, she seemed as though she were about to reply, but then she looked around the hallway and shook her head.

"Let's just say the fact that it didn't cut you is… interesting," was all she said, in the end.

I nodded, even though I had no idea what I was agreeing with.

"Well, I'd better get to Mr. Bumblebee's office, I

suppose." I may have started unexpectedly giving lip to teachers, but I wasn't about to start ignoring direct orders to go see the principal.

The Zoe look-alike tilted her head as though she expected me to do precisely that.

"You really respect *her* authority?" she asked.

I shrugged.

"I need to talk to him, anyway."

It was true. I had been meaning to talk to him sometime today about what I could do to keep Edik away from me, even if the police weren't going to cooperate. Just because either I, or the world, was going insane didn't mean I had to put up with Edik's bullshit.

I turned again and headed down the hall, not sure what had just happened or why it seemed so important. Not to mention why I was mesmerized by the eyes of a woman I'd just met.

"**H**EY! WAIT!" CAME the voice of the woman whose hands made my skin tingle.

"What?" I asked, turning slightly as I kept walking towards Albert's office.

"We need to talk," she said, her strides keeping pace with mine, even though she was a good three inches shorter than I was. Or would have been, if her black, combat-style boots hadn't had a two-inch heel.

"About what?" I asked, trying to focus on the hallway walls instead of on the warmth creeping up my skin as she drew closer.

"We shouldn't talk about it here," she said, grabbing my wrist.

The surge of warmth that spread up my arm and shot straight to my core was enough to stop me in my tracks. I swallowed, staring at where her hand touched my wrist, expecting to see… something that explained the reaction I was feeling, but it was just her skin touching mine.

"That's… weird," she said, clearing her throat and dropping my wrist.

"What exactly—"

Before I could ask any of the five million questions that jumped into my head, a familiar voice interrupted me.

"Vic, hey! I got to English late and heard you were sent to Bumblebee's office again. Need company?"

Seamus was a surprisingly welcome sight. I wouldn't have thought that seeing someone who had only recently revealed to me that he was a werewolf would make me feel less anxious, but I had to admit that, after the chaos of finding Edik waiting for me in first period physics and then being attacked by a teacher not five minutes into second period… Seamus' friendly, open expression made a few of the knots in my neck and shoulders relax.

"Go away, pup," the new girl snarled. "I have something important to discuss with her."

"The fuck?" I asked, my brain unable to keep my tongue from spewing forth whatever it conjured. "Why are you talking to him that way?"

"I don't play with dogs," she replied, as if that somehow explained things.

"I have no idea what you mean, but Seamus is my friend and he's walking me to the principal's office, so if you 'don't play with dogs' I guess that means you can take a long walk off a short pier."

I grabbed Seamus' arm, did my best to ignore the heat that coursed through me when I touched his skin, and dragged us both in the direction of the principal's office.

What the fuck is with me today? Has sleep deprivation made me the horniest person on the planet? It's like I can't touch people without wanting to jump their bones.

Seamus looked smug enough that I almost turned back to talk to the new kid. If he was getting possessive, then this friendship was going to be over before it even started. Ugh. I was probably reading too much into it. My brain was still fried from last night. There was too much bullshit going on. It wasn't even lunch time yet, and I was sooo done with this day.

Just as I had that thought, the new kid caught up to us and grabbed my arm again, but this time I ignored the fireworks inside me and kept trucking.

"Wait! Vic, stop walking! I need to talk to you about your brother."

Well, fuck. That did it. I shook free of her arm, let go of Seamus' elbow, turned towards the nearest exit, and ran.

I *DON'T HAVE a brother. I don't have a brother. I don't have a brother.*

Of course, you'd think, if I really didn't have a brother, that having said non-existent brother mentioned wouldn't be giving me a fucking panic attack. So, then, you'd wonder why I was sprinting—not walking, not running, SPRINT-ING, as fast as my limbs could propel me—out the nearest exit and into the street.

I stopped when I felt sunlight on my skin, inhaling a breath of clear Northern Arizona air while I took a moment to try to figure out why some new girl bringing up a brother I *didn't* have made me want to run away in a blind panic.

And then I instantly forgot about that, because a wolf and a panther came slamming out of the door I'd just sprinted through and before I could tell my brain not to panic, that the wolf was probably just

Seamus, I was sprinting again, as fast I could, towards home.

Part of my brain was taking this moment to remind me that running away from predators was a terrible idea, especially ones that had decent land speed, but it was too late. My limbs were already pumping, my blood was filled with adrenaline, and I was headed flat-out for home.

It belatedly occurred to me that leading wild animals to my house might not be the best idea, and I ducked down a side street lined with tiny wooden houses and lawns in various stages of disarray, hoping to distract or lose them.

They must have slowed a bit, because I didn't see them as I made yet another turn that would take me one more block out of my way before I beelined it back to my place.

By the time I reached my cul-de-sac there were no large predators in sight, and I had regained enough calm to convince myself that the wolf must have been Seamus, and thus it was unlikely that I was in any real danger. Still, try convincing *your* brain of that when you're staring at over three hundred pounds of raging panther and wolf running you down.

I took a deep breath as I approached my house, trying to let its barely familiar teal wood paneling and cedar-shingled roof bring me some kind of calm. I willed the pines that surrounded the property to lend me some strength, and hoped, rather desperately, that I was done with crazy for the day. I didn't even care that I was officially skipping more than half of the school day.

As I neared the front porch, I had almost convinced myself that I could go upstairs and rest for the remainder of the day, when a form appeared on my doorstep that made my blood run cold.

"My darling Victoria!"

"Fuck you, Eric," I muttered, getting ready to fight.

I T WAS PROBABLY childish to take delight in calling someone by a name they hated, but if anyone deserved it, the sparkle-fanged douchecanoe standing on my top step did.

Edik wasted no time in violating my personal space.

"Darling Victoria," he exclaimed again, reaching for me even as I settled into a fighting stance, "I've missed you since this mo—"

He didn't get to finish, because the moment his hand reached my shoulder I peeled it off of me and turned with him so that his weight and my momentum acted to take his center of gravity. Then I leaned with him and dropped my own center of gravity so that he had no choice but to launch head over heels into the scrub oak that adorned my front stoop.

"Victoria, how—"

I never heard what he was going to ask then, because at that exact moment three hundred pounds of black feline fury slammed into him and started tearing him up.

I had been preparing my next round of defense, but the arrival of unexpected feline backup gave me pause. Would the panther attack me, too, if I joined in? Was it here to help me, or just happy to attack whatever looked tasty?

My hesitation dissipated when a familiar snarl came from near my elbow and Seamus-as-wolf launched himself into the panther-diamond-toothed-asshat-melee happening in my scrub oak.

The panther seemed to be doing its best to coordinate its attacks with Seamus', although it was clear that Seamus didn't have much experience fighting with help, or maybe even fighting at all, as he kept getting in the panther's way.

That decided me, especially when Edik took a bite out of Seamus' shoulder and he started bleeding solidly from a gaping wound.

The panther and wolf were both attacking low, so while Edik dealt with them, I went in high, planning to start a series of kicks to Edik's head and shoulders, since he was preoccupied guarding his lower half and wouldn't have a chance to grab my legs. It would have been a solid plan of attack too, if Seamus hadn't lurched sideways and fallen into my planted leg, just after I'd shifted my weight and started the arc of a high kick. Too committed to the move to regain my balance, I toppled forward, and Edik didn't hesitate to catch me and wrap one arm around my throat.

"I do not like your friendth, Victoria," he mumbled into my ear, and I saw out of the corner of my eye that his clear, sparkly canines were entirely too long, and dripping somebody's blood.

I was already struggling against his hold, trying to gain enough purchase to let me knee him in the groin, or administer another head-butt, but he was holding me tight against him with one insanely strong arm, while still fighting the dodging and weaving panther with the other.

Seamus seemed to be losing steam, but he managed to get in one last lunge, causing the panther to shift course at the last second, and me to scream as the panther's teeth found the meat of my calf instead of whatever else they'd been aiming for.

And then the world went insane.

Suddenly my vision was reporting to my brain in a way that did not compute. Everything looked like I'd upped the frames per second rate on my video console, and the world was... not quite the right color. Moreover, my feet were no longer touching the ground.

I tried to scream, because Edik was now actually strangling me, since I couldn't find purchase on the ground beneath me, and I was suspended in his arms by the neck, but all that came out was a strange growl.

The fuck?

Panicked, I scrambled against Edik with everything I had, and was amazed when I felt claws unsheathe and drag against flesh. Edik screamed in agony and jumped away, releasing me, even as I turned and pivoted mid-air so that I landed on…

…all *four* legs?

Seriously. What. The. Fuck?

I barely noticed that Edik was running screaming into the neighbor's yard. I was too busy trying to figure out what in the seven hells had happened to me.

"Is your door locked?" a voice asked from nearby.

I turned, and saw the gorgeous new girl standing completely naked on my front step.

I tried to answer her, but a purr was all that escaped me.

Really, a purr? I mean, yeah, she was hot as hell, but I was just trying to say the door was open.

When that failed, I swayed my head up and down.

She stepped forward, turned the handle, and gestured inside.

"Come on, we shouldn't let anyone see us like this if we can help it."

Baffled by what the hell had just happened to my life, I followed a naked new girl and a limping Seamus-wolf into my house.

S SOON AS the door closed behind us I looked from Seamus to the new girl and back again, hoping that my face—whatever it looked like now—conveyed the full weight of my "what the everlasting fuck?!" attitude.

Seamus shifted back to human form and I had to take a moment to regain my composure.

What the hell? Did I seriously just lick my paw?

I stared at it in bafflement, not sure how to process any of this. I had paws. Four of them. They were large, seriously large... they splayed wide when I walked, and they were white, with maybe a hint of grey and some light spotting.

Curiosity getting the better of me, I padded upstairs to my bedroom, pushed my way past the door, and swung around to stand in front of the full-length mirror that hung down the back of it.

I sat down, stunned.

I was a snow leopard.

A snow leopard.

A motherfucking SNOW LEOPARD!!!

This was awesome!!!

I ran down the stairs, taking them in leaps, and landed excitedly at the bottom.

"I'M A FUCKING SNOW LEOPARD!" I screamed.

And then I looked down.

"Damn it. I'm human again."

Heat rose to my cheeks as I looked at Seamus and the new girl standing naked in my kitchen and re-alized that I, too, was bereft of clothing. I worked hard to tamp down the surge of attraction I felt for both of them. *Chill out, body, now is REALLY not the time!* I turned metaphorical tail and ran upstairs again. Halfway up the stairs I realized that my clothes were probably lying in a pile on my front step, but I was soooo not going back downstairs and *outside* butt naked to get them. I headed to my room instead.

When I came back down I was fully clothed, and I carried a baggy pair of sweats and a t-shirt for Seamus and an extra pair of jeans and a tank top for the new girl.

"You're both welcome to stay naked if you're… er… more comfortable that way, but… well, in case you're not, I brought some clothes down."

I tried not to blush while I handed the clothes out.

"I didn't realize snow leopards were so shy," the new girl said, taking the clothes but not looking like she was in any rush to put them on.

Seamus cleared his throat, and I was relieved to see he'd put the pants on immediately.

"She wasn't raised in a were community," he said, as if that explained everything.

I shrugged.

"Seriously, I have nothing against nudity, I just… I wasn't comfortable, so I thought I'd offer you the same amenities. You're welcome to stay as you are…. What's your name, by the way?"

"I'm Sol," she said, extending her hand to shake mine. "Short for Soledad."

"Nice to meet you, Sol," I said, returning the handshake. "This is Seamus."

Seamus reached his hand out and Sol sneered at it briefly, then looked away.

"Wow," I said, not liking where this was going. "That was shitty. What's your problem?"

Apparently, I was all out of diplomacy for the day.

Sol shrugged and walked out of the room holding the jeans and tank I'd brought her. She didn't head for the door, so I didn't think she was leaving. I assumed she had just decided to change out of sight. Why she bothered, when she'd just been standing naked in front of us for five minutes, was anyone's guess.

"What the fuck was that, Seamus?" I asked, as soon as she was gone.

"I don't think she likes me," he said, glaring after Sol's retreating form.

"Clearly not. That's not what I mean. What the fuck just happened out there?!" I gestured wildly to the front door.

"Oh that," he said. "Looks like you found your were form."

"My what? What does that mean?"

"Well, as you so accurately shouted when you got down the stairs, you're a motherfucking snow leopard."

His smile was entirely too smug for my liking.

"What does that mean? How is that even possible? WHAT IS HAPPENING TO ME?!"

Of course, that moment, the moment when I was basically falling into full-blown panic mode, was the moment that Sol came back from the bathroom.

"Gatita, don't worry. Nothing is wrong, you're just doing what you're supposed to do. You're a were, just like me, somewhat like your doggy pal here. You have an animal form that you can call on at will. Although, I will admit, it usually takes us a while longer to learn how to call and dismiss our animal selves so quickly. You seem particularly adept at it."

I looked between Sol and Seamus.

"That explains precisely NOTHING. How is it possible that I'm a were anything? How could I not know this?! Didn't you say it was genetic?"

That last one I directed firmly at Seamus. Last night, when I'd been peppering him with questions, trying to convince myself that werewolves didn't exist even with the evidence staring me in the face, he'd explained that the condition wasn't transferred by bite, it was genetic. You were only a were if your parents were weres, and your animal was likely to be the same animal that your parents called on, although there were exceptions.

"You lied to me," I said, staring him down. "My parents weren't weres. I would have known if they were, they would never have hidden that from me, and I've never changed before. Until... until she BIT me!"

I glared at both of them.

"It is genetic, Gatita. My biting you didn't do anything except call your animal to you for the first time. Our animal forms require another were's bite to bring them across. Contact with another were's saliva is like a neon sign calling your animal over. Like calls to like."

"WHAT DOES THAT EVEN MEAN?!"

None of this made sense. Don't get me wrong, I'd spent my entire childhood and early adolescence waiting for my damned owl to arrive and tell me I was special, magical, somehow privy to a different world in which dragons were actually REAL, but this was ridiculous. I was an adult now, or would be in a week or so, and I knew as well as anyone that magic wasn't real, as much as I wanted it to be. I couldn't be a wereleopard. My parents would have told me. Also, physics. I mean, come on. How on earth could I be both a human and a snow leopard at the same time? That just didn't make sense.

Judging by the looks on Sol and Seamus' faces, I must have said some portion of that out loud.

"Gatita, physics is precisely how this whole thing works. I'm not one of the folks who research this kind of thing, but the way you access your were is through dark matter, at least that's what the latest scientific journals are claiming. It's not the kind of thing I pay attention to."

That was a non-explanation if ever I'd heard one, but it was clear that Sol wasn't super up-to-date on the physics stuff. I'd have to ask someone else about how dark matter allowed me to have a snow leopard form. There were plenty of other questions fighting for my attention instead.

"But my parents…" I argued feebly.

"Now that one, Gatita, I can easily explain. Your parents certainly knew you're a were. They were both weres themselves, and they probably told you about it, too, at least early on, but… after your brother went missing…"

"My brother…"

"I didn't know you had a brother, Vic."

"I don't… I didn't… I don't know…"

I suddenly had a raging headache, one that felt like my skull was about to split.

"We're going to need tea, I think," Sol said, fumbling through my cupboards and pulling out the kettle and my assorted tea collection.

"Gatita, I don't know how to say this any other way, so I'm just going to say it," she said, filling the kettle and placing it on the stove top. "You're brother is alive and I know where to find him."

And *that* was when I passed out.

T HE TEAKETTLE STILL hadn't boiled when I opened my eyes to find Seamus holding my hand and whimpering at me even though he was in human form.

"I'm ok," I said, shaking him off and sitting up slowly. "Just… I'm not sure, actually, my head feels like I'm recovering from a bender." I'd never actually been on a bender, but the one time I'd gotten drunk at a cousin's wedding it had felt kind of like this the morning after.

Seamus helped me to my feet, despite my best efforts to shake him off, and I couldn't decide if I was appreciative of his concern or peeved by the coddling. Honestly, I was shaky enough that I was leaning towards appreciative. The peeved part of me was probably a holdover from his interference in the fight. Where he'd gotten in my way and wound up causing Sol to bite me. Which had turned me into a freaking snow leopard.

"Did I hallucinate that?" I asked, even as I checked out my ankle and found it devoid of any sign that it had been bitten by a three hundred pound panther. My brain seemed to be ignoring the fact that the run-up to that question had all been in my head.

"Hallucinate what, Gatita?" Sol asked, handing me a cup of Earl Grey. "Drink this, it will help with the headache."

"Did you infuse it with eye of newt or something?" I asked, eyeing the cup warily.

Sol laughed.

"No, caffeine helps with headaches, that's all. I'd make you a coffee, but I don't see a coffee maker, so…"

I shrugged and took a sip of the Earl Grey, not bothering to mention my aero press—which was probably still in my backpack from the weekend anyway—or the fact that there was a coffee pot hidden somewhere in the pile of boxes I had yet to unpack in the garage. Honestly, just doing something as normal as sipping tea helped me let go of some of the tension in my neck and shoulders.

"Me turning into a snow leopard," I asked, trying to get back to the subject at hand, instead of getting sidetracked by home remedies. "Did I actually turn into a snow leopard, or was that just a freaky hallucination? I don't have any signs of a bite on my leg."

"Yes, you turned into a snow leopard. The signs of it disappeared because you shifted afterwards, the bite was small, and shifting speeds up healing," Seamus said. Then he smiled. "See, I told you, you aren't just a normal human."

The look on his face made it sound like it should have been the best news in the world, but even though turning into a snow leopard was basically a childhood dream come true… the whole thing just felt like a betrayal.

"How is it possible my parents never told me about this?"

Seamus looked at Sol quizzically.

"I told you she might not remember," Sol said, making me even more confused.

"What? What am I not remembering?"

"Vic, Sol said there were some powerful mage spells put on you and your parents when you were a kid."

"What?! Why?"

That didn't sound good. None of this sounded good, and my headache was coming back with a vengeance.

"Do you remember what we were talking about just before you passed out?" Seamus asked. His voice sounded gentle, like he was about to pull off a Band-Aid but wanted to lessen the sting.

I tried to think back to what we'd talked about before I'd blacked out, but it just made my headache rage, and I couldn't think through the pain anymore. I cradled my head in my arms and focused on not vomiting.

"This isn't going to work. The spell is too strong. She's just going to keep passing out every time we bring it up," Sol said, though I could barely hear her over the pounding in my ears.

"What if she shifts and we tell her snow leopard?"

"That might work," Sol said, after a pause. "If the spell was only cast on her human form, her snow leopard might be free of it. It won't work if it was a spirit binding, but if it was just a corporeal spell, that should do the trick." She hesitated for a moment. "Nice thinking, puppy."

If I'd been in less pain, I might have given her a talking-to about backhanded compliments. As it was, the headache was still raging, and besides, Seamus could probably take care of himself. I might have heard a growl, but it was hard to tell over the sound of my skull being stabbed repeatedly with a knife—metaphorically speaking.

"Vic, can you hear me?" Sol asked.

I nodded, and then instantly regretted it. Mental note: DO. NOT. MOVE. HEAD.

"Vic, can you manage a shift? Do you have any idea how to call on your snow leopard right now?"

I did not shake my head, but talking seemed like an impossibility with my jaw seizing with pain, so I just whimpered a bit and hoped that got my point across.

"Ok, Seamus is going to talk you through it."

I had no idea why Seamus was being voluntold to take care of me, but I was in no position to argue or second-guess.

"Ok, Vic… just… try to relax, if you can. Can you remember what it felt like to be a snow leopard? Try to imagine it, if you can. What was different from the way you normally move, smell, see, taste, balance? Try to picture those things, and then… sort of… *will* them into being."

Sol snorted, and I wondered if she thought Seamus' instructions were lacking in some way. I tried to do what Seamus said, but the pain was too much for my concentration.

"Vic," Sol said, her voice getting closer to where my head was cradled in my own arms. "If you manage the shift, the headache should go away."

Suddenly, I found the will to concentrate. At that moment, I would have done *anything* to make the headache go away, and damned if I wasn't going to figure out how to turn into a snow leopard right that fucking moment.

I tried recalling the details that Seamus had suggested, but it was hard to come up with things like sight, sound, and smell right then. My brain was overtaken with pain, and those kinds of details were hard to recall even on a good day. So I focused on the parts of me that didn't hurt. The sensation of having four paws, the agility to right myself midfall, the balance of a giant, glorious snow leopard tail.

Then, suddenly, I was calling on my tail, paws, and agility to balance me as I slid from a precarious perch on a stool and kitchen island and fell to the floor.

I smiled delightedly when I landed on four paws, and then smiled wider still when I realized the damned headache was gone.

"Is she *purring*?" Seamus asked, his face bewildered.

Sol just laughed.

I looked at them both expectantly. I wanted to know about whatever it was I had forgotten.

"Ok, Vic, *now* do you remember what we were talking about before you passed out?"

Oddly, I still had access to those memories. Which was weird, because those memories were in human form and currently I was a very large feline. I ignored the disconnect and focused on the memories themselves… we had been talking about my parents and them not telling me I was a were, and then Sol had started to explain why and….

I sat down with a thud, my tail flipping angrily around me as the weight of memory hit me. My brother… I had a brother, and he was still alive, and Sol knew where he was.

And then the floodgates opened. Images from my childhood that had been blocked, or that I had repressed. A little boy, my age, my height, similar features, just… a boy, and clever, and mischievous, and we'd had soooo many adventures together, and…

Did snow leopards cry? Or… I shut my mouth and looked at Seamus and Sol, and the horrified looks on their faces confirmed that I had been making a truly terrible noise.

So I focused on the feeling of tears in my eyes, and grief in my throat, and… suddenly I was sitting in the middle of my kitchen floor, naked and sobbing.

"I REMEMBERED HIM!" I cried, standing up and reaching for the kitchen counter, ignoring the pile of my clothes that lay on the floor beside the stool.

"Good. Then the spell is gone."

"No." I shook my head, grateful that the headache seemed to still be gone, even though I was back in human form. "I mean, I remembered him before, when I was a kid. They tried to charm us all, they DID charm us, but… it didn't quite take on me at first. After they took him, my parents tried to get him back, tried and tried, but nothing worked, and then… then we moved, and my parents told me I couldn't talk about Trevor anymore, and then… they had us all charmed, all of us, and… they stopped talking about him. It wasn't like he was dead, they pretended that he had never existed, that I'd never had a brother, that my *twin* didn't even exist, but it didn't work on me… not at first, and I kept trying to make them remember, and they kept telling me I was making up stories, and…"

My breath caught in my chest as the memories hit me, one after another.

"They sent me to see a psychiatrist. They had me treated… and… I stopped. I didn't want them to put me away somewhere, and I didn't want them to be so mad at me all the time, so finally… I just stopped talking about him, and… eventually, I couldn't remember if he was real or not, he felt more like something I had made up…. My mom always talked about the day they tried to take me as though that was all that had happened, as though they'd never taken Trevor, of course, because he didn't exist… and then…"

My breath hitched on a sob before I managed to speak again.

"I forgot about him. I stopped talking about him, and, slowly, I started to believe he'd never existed. Eight years of memories… how could I forget about him? How? How did I forget my twin brother?"

Seamus patted my back, and caught me as my legs started to give out again. I let him support me for a moment before I settled myself on one of the stools. Then I remembered that I was still naked. I ran the back of my wrist across my face to get the worst of the tears and snot, then grabbed my clothes and rushed upstairs to put them on again.

When I came back downstairs, Seamus and Sol were standing on opposite sides of my kitchen island, sharing what looked like an awkward silence.

"So… do cats and dogs not get along in the magic world, either?" I asked, trying to lighten the mood. Sol merely shrugged in response, but Seamus grinned.

"I like *you* just fine," he said.

The sincerity of his smile made me smile in return.

"You're alright in my book too, Seamus," I said, bumping shoulders with him on my way back to my tea mug. "At least for now. Don't show up in my room uninvited or anything."

Seamus growled, even though he was still in human form.

"No worries on that front," he muttered.

I sighed, taking a sip of my tea as I sat down at the kitchen island once more.

"Vic, when you talked about your brother disappearing… you kept saying 'they' took him. Do you know who 'they' is?" Seamus asked, pulling up the stool beside me.

I shook my head.

"Not really. My parents knew, I think, but… I don't think they told me, or if they did, I'm not sure I understood. I was only eight. Sol, you said you know where he is. Do you also know who took him?"

Sol nodded.

"I do. He's in Bolivia, and I know who put him there, and why. Are you ready to hear any of that?"

I took a deep breath, letting the long-suppressed memories of my brother resurface. Letting the kidnapping come back to me was hard. It was difficult to relive the terror I'd felt as an eight-year-old watching my brother get taken away.

"Shotgun!" Trev called, rushing towards the car, the way he always did, as if Mom ever let either of us ride up front.

"Trev, wait up!" I called from behind him, tugging Mom along so she would hurry up. Trev and I were both excited to get home and test out the new gaming console we'd just gotten. No more playing at Frida's house! Wii bowling nights could happen in our very own living room!

"Come on, Mom! This is going to be the best birthday ever!"

Mom laughed as I tugged her along, dragging her feet, probably just to give me more of a challenge.

"GET AWAY FROM ME!"

My head shot up, and Mom and I were both suddenly running flat-out towards the car. Two men had grabbed Trevor and were wrestling him into a nondescript white van. Trev wasn't going without a fight though, he was flailing and kicking like a wild animal. I heard one of the men grunt in pain as we got closer to the car.

Then Mom turned into the biggest bird I'd ever seen, and launched herself at the men holding Trevor.

"LET GO OF MY BROTHER!!" I screamed, over and over again, while the two men holding him shoved him into the back of the cargo van, and my mom screeched and threw herself at them repeatedly. A third person emerged from the front of the van and came running towards me then, and I screamed until my lungs were on fire. Mom dove at the woman, just before she reached me, digging her talons into the woman's face, causing her to scream even more loudly than I had.

The woman turned and ran. Probably because the white van was pulling away.

Mom flew after it, throwing herself at the windows, but the woman turned back in my direction and I ran away from her, screaming for help. I didn't see what happened to her, but I heard her scream as I dove into the elevator that would take me back to the main floor of the parking garage and the entrance to the mall. Mom landed next to me a moment later. As the doors closed, she returned to her human form, naked and sobbing.

I was crying again by the time the memory was over, but I took comfort in knowing that I was about to find out who those people had worked for.

Finally, I nodded, wondering how much time had passed since Sol had asked her question.

"Yes, Sol, I would like to know who took my brother."

Just as Sol opened her mouth to answer, I heard a knock on the door.

I glanced at the clock on my microwave. 2:41PM.

"Who the hell would that be?" I asked, standing up and heading for the door.

"Wait!" Sol, shouted. "It could be a trap!"

"A trap?" I asked, still walking for the door. Who would come to trap me in my own house? Hell, who even knew where I lived?

I walked to the door, worried that it might be Edik, but deciding that, just in case Sol wasn't crazy, I would check the peephole before I opened it.

What I saw made my brain skip so hard that I opened the door before I'd even had time to think about it.

"Hey, Vic," Trevor said, standing with his hands in his pockets, looking for all the world like a six-foot-tall, dark, handsome, unsure puppy.

I could barely see through all the tears, but I launched myself at him before he had a chance to back away, and wrapped him in a bone-crunching hug.

"Trev! Holy shit!! Is it really you?"

I pushed back, still holding his shoulders, and looked into the bright golden eyes that looked so much like mine, except for the color. His eyes looked darker, in a way, like they'd seen a lot of suffering in the past ten years, but… well, they probably matched mine in that respect. So many things about him reminded me of what I saw in the mirror every day. Hell, he even wore his black hair long like mine. I hadn't seen him in 10 years, and he'd changed just as much as I had in that time, but… I would have known him anywhere.

I wrapped him in another hug, and this time, he actually wrapped his arms around me in return.

"I missed you too, Vic," he whispered into my hair.

I held onto him for another minute. I couldn't help myself. It was like the longer I held him, the more real he became. He even smelled right. Eventually, I pulled back again and smiled at him.

"You should come inside," I said, gesturing to the door that still hung open behind me. "This is your house too."

Trev shrugged and followed me inside.

I couldn't let go of him completely, so I kept his hand in mine. It was warm, dry, and lightly calloused.

"Trev, this is Seamus, he's… a werewolf from my English class," I said, wondering when my life had turned into a fucking J.K. Rowling novel. "And this is Soledad, a werepanther from… well, I'm not entirely sure where, but I think she was about to explain."

Trev's grip on my hand tightened, and he drew me behind him.

"She doesn't need to explain," Trev said, his voice dropping. "I know exactly where she's from."

And then my brother burst into flames and threw himself at Sol.

"**N**o, Trev, wait!" I called out, as Sol shifted deftly into her sleek black panther form, all the while dodging and weaving against my brother's fiery attacks.

As my eyes adjusted to the scene, I saw that he hadn't actually burst into flames so much as turned into a phoenix. Which I supposed amounted to the same thing, since a phoenix was basically just a big bird that caught fire.

"TREV! Seriously! She was just about to explain how she knew where you were before you knocked on the door. Can you just give her a chance to talk before you burn her to death?!"

The show that Trev and Sol were putting on was a good one, and it was nice to see that my brother had some impressive weapons at his disposal, but Sol had clearly been trained to fight by someone who knew what they were doing, and she was doing an excellent job of dodging Trev's attacks, countering just enough to give herself space without doing any damage to him.

Seamus took a few steps back from the fiery kitchen drama and stood next to me.

"I really need to learn how to fight," he admitted, as we watched Trev and Sol go after each other. "You and Sol didn't need me in the fight against Edik. I only made things worse."

I nodded. "Yeah, but your heart was in the right place." I sighed. "And anyway, there are lots of ways to be useful without learning to fight. The only reason I've been training for the past ten years is because of what happened to Trev… even though my parents pretended it was because of the 'attempt' to kidnap me…. I can teach you a few things if you want, though. My sensei in Colorado had me helping to teach some of the beginner classes before I left."

Seamus nodded. We both watched the teakettle get knocked off the stove top and go crashing to the floor.

"It's a good thing that's stainless steel," I mused.

Seamus raised an eyebrow at me.

"Are you… going to stop them?" he asked.

I shrugged.

"Trevor hasn't killed her, and if he had been planning a fatal attack I think she would be dead by now. Moreover, Sol has clearly been going out of her way not to hurt him. That can't have escaped his notice. Whatever beef he has with Sol will probably be out of his system in another minute or two."

"You sound pretty confident for someone who hasn't seen her brother in ten years," he said.

I smiled.

"He's still my twin," I said. "The only person I know better is me."

"But if he's been held captive that whole time…" Seamus took a deep breath and ran his hand along the back of his neck. "Don't you think it's possible he's changed in ways you can't understand?"

I nodded, the smile falling from my face.

"I'm sure he has, Seamus, but… I still know that if he were trying to hurt her, this fight would have been over a long time ago. I don't know who the better fighter is, but…" I gestured vaguely at the two figures dodging and weaving in front of us, "they're both clearly good. Which means if they were trying to harm one another, it would be over by now. Instead… no one has even drawn blood."

"Then why are they still fighting?" Seamus asked.

"Because Trev is fucking furious, though I'm not sure why."

When Sol batted at Trevor hard enough that he backed into my cupboard and set my coffee stash on fire, I drew the line.

"THAT'S ENOUGH!" I shouted, running forward to put out the flames. "Damn it, Trev! If I'd wanted it to taste like burnt asshole I'd have bought dark roast!"

Sol and Trevor backed away from each other and looked at me with similar expressions of amusement, even though it was kind of difficult to read flaming bird face.

"Do you two want to explain what the fuck is going on now that you've had your little sparring match? Do you know each other?"

Trev resumed his human form, and I realized that eight years of shared bath time had not prepared me for seeing my eighteen-year-old brother naked. I took a deep breath and stared him in the eyes.

"Do you want to borrow some sweatpants?" I asked, glancing at the charred remains of the jeans and t-shirt Trev had been wearing when he walked in.

He nodded, and I pointed upstairs.

"I'm not going anywhere while she's here to spread lies," he hissed.

I shrugged.

"I promise not to believe a single word she says until you come back downstairs."

Trev glared at me.

Sol shifted to human and smiled. The gesture was decidedly feline, even though she no longer had whiskers. "I promise not to speak until you return, Avito."

"First door on the left," I said.

By the time he came back down, wearing a pair of sweatpants with my old high school's mascot on the leg, Sol had once more donned the clothes I'd given her earlier.

"So, please enlighten me as to why you two couldn't resist pretending to fight the second you saw each other."

Trev scoffed.

"I wasn't pretending… but when I noticed she was going out of her way not to hurt me… I laid off my more devastating attacks."

"And I didn't come here to kill anyone," Sol said. "Although if that damned vampire shows up again, I may change my mind."

I chuckled.

"Only after I kill him first."

Trev glanced between us.

"What vampire is this?" he asked.

I shook my head. "One who isn't even worth the time to discuss right now. Focus power, people. What the hell is going on between you two?"

Trev sighed.

"It's nothing personal… with, Soledad, did you say?"

I nodded.

"We've never met before, but… she smells like MOME."

"She smells like what?" I asked.

"MOME," Trevor said, saying a word that rhymed with "home" and looking at me like I'd said the sky was orange.

"The Ministry of Magical Entities," Sol clarified.

Trev kept looking at me as though I were growing a second head.

"How do you not know what MOME is?" he asked. "That's like never having heard of Congress."

I sighed.

"Yeah, so about that…. After you were taken, Mom, Dad, and I had our memories messed with, and they pretended we weren't…" I gestured between us futilely, "whatever the fuck we are."

"Huh?"

"Vic had never heard of anything from our world until I told her I was a werewolf last night," Seamus said.

"This morning," I corrected. "It was late enough that it was technically this morning."

Trev looked stunned beyond words.

"I have never heard of MOME, and, until about 30 minutes ago, I thought that you didn't exist and that I was a normal human."

Then I smiled, as a single happy thought struck me.

"But I just turned into a SNOW LEOPARD for the first time ever! So, I'm pretty stoked about that."

Trev smiled too.

"Well, that's fun. I had wondered what animal you'd wind up with. Our family has lots to choose from."

"Choose?" I asked.

Trev ignored me and turned to glare at Sol, even though she hadn't made a sound.

"We can talk about that later. She should explain why she knew where I was and why she's even here."

I would have argued, because every damned thing that came out of Trev's mouth spawned about 500 new questions in my mind, but I also wanted to know what Sol had to do with all of this, and why Trev had wanted to kill her because she 'smelled like MOME.'"

Sol cleared her throat and sat down on the stool she'd been perched on before Trev got here, but Seamus, Trev, and I remained standing.

"It's reasonable that you don't trust me right now," she said, taking a sip from one of the tea cups that had miraculously managed to survive the kitchen brawl. "Because I do, as Trevor implied, work for MOME."

That revelation caused Trev to hiss like an angry ostrich and Seamus to gasp, but I was still lost as to what the big deal was.

"Vic," Sol said, as though understanding my confusion, "MOME is the organization that governs the magical community. It's the police force, the legislative force, the bureaucratic branch, everything most governments do, all rolled into one."

"Only where other governments are filled with elected officials, and vary from region to region, MOME is self-selected, and is the self-proclaimed governing body for magical entities all over the *world*," Trev gritted out, between clenched jaws.

I took a moment to put together the few tidbits that I understood about the magical world and realization came slowly.

"And it was MOME that decided to take an eight-year-old boy from his family?" I asked, as the horror sank in. "WHY?!"

Trev snorted in derision.

"Oh, they weren't just after me, Vic. They would have taken you too, if Mom hadn't fought them off so well."

My stomach turned, but I repeated the question. "Why?" I turned to Sol, who looked decidedly uncomfortable. She swallowed.

"They deem certain younglings to be… dangers, to themselves and others. Both you and your brother were on a watchlist. I don't know why, exactly, they decided to take you then, since I've only been working at MOME for about two years, but last night my unit leader put me on a flight to come here and… retrieve you."

Trev squared off, putting himself between me and Sol, but I grabbed his shoulder and pulled him behind me.

"Cool your jets, Trev, I can handle the panther." I wasn't entirely sure that was true. Sol seemed like a pretty accomplished fighter, especially in her panther form, but I knew I could do at least as well as Trev could, and have I mentioned how much I hate overprotective males? Twin brothers were no exception.

"So, why didn't you just nab me back in Rebuke's class and take me off to… wherever it is you're supposed to drag me?"

Sol looked around the room, taking in the ceiling and the windows in particular. Then she shook her head.

"I'm not at liberty to say."

For some reason that didn't piss Trev off the way I expected it to. He turned to me and mouthed the word "bugs."

I nodded, finally understanding Sol's exaggerated inspection of our ceiling.

"Ok. So, what *can* you tell us?" I asked.

"We shouldn't stay here very long," Sol replied.

"Which is precisely what someone would say if they were trying to get us to accompany them back to the bad guys' hideout," I muttered.

At least Seamus laughed.

"Vic, where are Mom and Dad?" Trev asked, after a moment of awkward silence.

I felt like I'd been stabbed in the chest.

"They… they're…" For some reason, I couldn't bring myself to say the word dead. So instead I copped out with, "they disappeared in the Indian Ocean."

Trev's eyes filled with tears, and I moved to him and wrapped him in another giant hug. This time, he didn't hesitate before hugging me back.

I already knew that, but I had to make it sound like I didn't have access to our file, said a voice inside my head that was not my own.

I startled, but Trev held me tight and didn't let me back away.

We both have a lot more magic now than when we were kids, Vic. Don't you remember when we tried to talk to each other's minds back then?

I was about to say no, but then the memories came flooding back to me. We'd tried, over and over again for years, but the best we'd managed was to sense the other person's emotions. Even then, we'd never been sure that it was magic and not just… knowing each other really well.

Are you telling me this really works? I asked.

Trev laugh/cried into my hair.

Hey, try not to snot me too badly. There are hot people watching us.

But of course that just made him laugh/cry harder.

What do we do to get out of this? I want to know what happened to you. Can you talk about that here? I had a million questions, and I wasn't sure I could keep any of them back now that I could just think them at Trev.

Yeah. MOME already knows that, so their listening spells won't tell them anything they don't already know, but when we get to the end of the story I'm going to have to lie, or we're going to have to go somewhere else. Sol's right, though. They'll have figured out that I'm here, which means we need to go somewhere else soon.

Can they see us? Or only hear us? I asked.

It depends on how long they've been monitoring you, but based on the fact that Sol only showed up here today, she probably only had time to set up listening devices.

Wait, she's the one that set them up? Why do we even trust her at all, then?

Well, we don't. But, she might have useful information, and she didn't grab you when she had an easy chance, so...

His thoughts trailed off for a moment and I decided there was nothing for it but to give it a shot.

Ok... I think I have a plan, I replied into Trev's mind, even though I could have easily said that bit aloud, because, why the fuck not? Everything else in my life was completely insane, so why wouldn't I be communicating telepathically with my twin brother who I thought was dead/never existed?

I backed away from Trevor and started miming to Seamus that we should go for a walk to his house. He nodded, and we all headed for the door.

Just as we got to the front step, Gwen popped into existence right in front me.

"Jesus fuck, Gwen! Don't do that. You scared me. What are you doing here?"

Gwen frowned.

"You're all needed elsewhere," she said, before somehow grabbing onto all four of us and then winking us all out of existence.

"**W**HAT THE HELL just happened?" Trev asked, over the howling wind.

"That was Gwen," I said, as if that explained everything. I looked at all three of my companions—Gwen, of course, was nowhere in sight—and realized that Sol and Seamus were just as confused as my brother.

"She's… well… the short explanation is that she's the one who first tipped me off that this was going to be a weird week."

That was probably the understatement of the century, but, well… the long explanation probably stretched credulity even amongst a bunch of were-creatures.

"Where are we?" Seamus asked, beginning to shiver.

I looked around. We were standing on a granite outcropping that kept us above the snow that covered the slope on which we stood, surrounded by steep, rocky peaks covered in more snow.

"The Andes?" I guessed, my teeth chattering. It could have been the Rockies, but… there was too much snow for September in the Rockies. September in the Andes, though… yeah, this looked about right.

"Everyone needs to shift," Sol said. "There's a place we can shelter near here, but this cold works quickly. Follow me."

Without waiting for anyone to object, Sol shifted to her panther form and started off down the hill. As tempting as it was to make a fuss about how we were suddenly in the Andes and why the fuck were we so close to a place that only Sol knew well… it was too fucking cold.

Seamus had already shifted by the time I had wished myself warmly wrapped in the thick fur of my snow leopard fervently enough to feel it suddenly surrounding me.

Being a snow leopard was the coolest.

Seriously. I was so warm. This might be the Andes, but the Andes had nothing on the Himalayas. Suddenly, I was in no particular rush to get to shelter, but as everyone else was trotting downhill at a decent clip behind Sol, I followed.

Of course, Trev caught up to Sol immediately, since he was flying, but Seamus was only a few meters ahead of me and I couldn't resist the temptation to race him down the hill. I nipped him playfully on the shoulder as I ran up alongside him, and then put on a surge of speed to close the distance between us and Sol. I could feel Seamus surge behind me to keep up, and he let out a competitive howl as we both hurtled over the snow-covered rocks that lay between us and our quarry.

Seamus, in wolf form, had much longer legs than I did as a snow leopard, and he would surely beat me in any long-distance race when we were on four legs, but for a short race over mountainous terrain…

He was sooo going down.

The terrain was uneven at best, with surprise boulders shooting up in front of us and small cliffs dropping away beneath us at every turn. I became hyper-focused, aware of every shift in terrain before I even had a chance to consciously process it, my body simply reacting to my surroundings in a way that I couldn't possibly replicate as a human. Sudden shifts of weight and balance were easy, my tail gliding effortlessly behind me to act as a counterbalance whenever necessary, my legs somehow able to shift mid-fall whenever the earth disappeared beneath me, able to orient themselves to whatever surface became my next foothold.

It was as though the earth were just an extension of my paws. I had never been in the Andes before, but every rock, snowdrift, and bit of patchy mountain scrub called out its familiar presence to me, and my body simply reacted.

Before I knew it, I was neck and neck with Sol and about to pull ahead of her. That was when I slowed up to circle back and check on Seamus. It didn't make any sense to try to outrun Sol, since she was the one who knew where we were going. Luckily, Seamus wasn't injured or anything, he was just stranded on one of the smallish cliffs that I had simply jumped over at full speed.

Damn, it was good to be a cat!

I quickly scaled the ledge and sat next to him. He was still in wolf form, staring frustratedly at the cliff, which occupied a large section of the hillside and would take a while to traverse if he didn't want to climb down the face.

I shifted to human and belatedly remembered that my clothes didn't shift with me.

"Want to down-climb it as a human?" I asked, already starting to shiver.

Seamus glared at me with his amber wolf eyes and huffed a bit.

"Well, do you want to follow me down, then? I promise to go slow this time."

Seamus nodded.

I happily shifted back to my snow leopard and started my descent, but this time, instead of running flat-out, I picked my way carefully down the sheer rock wall, making sure to select ledges that were big enough for wolf paws, and only making movements that would accommodate a wolf's somewhat more rigid center of gravity.

This time, when I got to the bottom, Seamus was right behind me. With another playful howl, he took off towards Sol and Trevor in the distance. I let out a yowl of challenge and followed close on his heels.

~~~

When we got to Sol's cabin, we were all a bit out of breath, even Trevor, which was weird since he had been flying and had needed to circle back a few times to make sure he didn't leave us all in the dust.

"It's the altitude," Sol said, after we'd all filed, panting, into a tiny wooden cabin perched precar-
~~~

iously on the side of the mountain we'd all just descended, surrounded by nothing more than a bit of mountain scrub and some boulders. "We're at around 6,000 meters. It gets to anyone who's not from here, or even those of us who haven't run at altitude in a long time."

Sol was, of course, naked as she said this, and busy rifling through a closet in the one bedroom that opened off of the living/dining/kitchen area, which constituted the majority of the cabin's square footage, aside from a rather large porch that clung to the top of the cliff ledge opposite the cabin's front door. None of us had bothered to carry our clothes down the mountainside, and we all stood naked and shivering in the common area waiting for Sol to kit us out.

Sol indiscriminately tossed clothing at us from inside the closet. Long wool underwear tops and bottoms, snow pants, coats… nothing terribly comfortable, but plenty that was warm. I grabbed the first thing that looked like it would fit and started pulling on layers. In a few minutes, we were all wearing enough clothing to be toasty, despite the lack of insulation in the tiny cabin and the swiftly plunging temperature outside.

Since I was the first one outfitted from the closet ransack, I set about starting a fire in the wood stove that acted as the center of the small living/dining/cooking area. The furnishings in the cabin were sparse—two low wooden couches with blankets piled up on them to make them comfortable and two large chairs. No real table to speak of, but a few small side tables next to the chairs and couches. A battered-looking upright bass leaned in one corner, looking somewhat worse for wear, and bright, woven tapestries hung on the walls, while a large alpaca rug covered most of the floor. Everything centered around the wood stove, as you might expect in a place that didn't have central heating.

Once the kettle was heating on top of the wood stove and we were all settled on the floor around it, Sol spoke again.

"We can speak freely here. MOME doesn't know about this place."

Trev's eyebrow rose, and Seamus and I looked between him and Sol for clarification.

"Why would you want a place that MOME doesn't know about, if you work for them?" Trev asked.

"Because," Sol said, taking a deep breath before continuing, "I have been working for MOME for the past two years as part of a larger plan to help take MOME down from the inside."

For a long moment, the howling wind outside was the only sound.

"Wait, what?" Trev and I said in unison, while Seamus merely stared wide-eyed at Sol.

"I know it sounds far-fetched, but my family… we're a big family, and well connected. My Abuelita has never liked the way MOME interferes with her business, and… well, we have some very personal reasons to want MOME to go down."

Knowing what I already knew about MOME and what they'd done to my own family, I didn't have a hard time believing that, but…

"It strikes me as more than a tiny bit suspicious that you're trusting us with that information when you haven't even known us for a full day," Trev said.

I nodded.

Seamus was silent.

Sol sighed again.

"I know," she said. "This isn't how I'd hoped things would go down, but now… I don't know that crazy redhead who teleported us here, and for the record I was under the impression that a teleport that far was impossible, but here we are, less than ten kilometers away from MOME's South American Headquarters, and—"

"What?!" Trev and I shouted at the same moment, though perhaps for different reasons.

"We're incredibly close to the Bolivian offices. My Abuelita's territory runs right alongside theirs.

I don't know why your friend brought us here. I was hoping to have a few days of helping you evade MOME's other agents to help bring you over to my side. I had a tidy little plan all in place, knowing what MOME was likely to throw at us and how helping you avoid it would make it easier for you to trust me…. But here we are, so what's the point in waiting?"

Unable to process everything Sol had just dropped on us, I turned to Seamus.

"Seamus, it occurs to me that you just kind of got dragged into all this. What are your feelings about MOME?"

Seamus shrugged.

"No one I know is a huge fan of them. We hear stories of the kind of crap that they pull all the time, but no one in my family has been personally affected by it…. That I know of, anyway."

Something in his face told me there was more to the story than what he'd just said, but far be it from me to press someone to relive whatever trauma an agency like MOME might have put them through. I took a minute to process what I'd heard so far. It was hard to be thrown into all of this and know how to feel about it. I had very strong feelings about an organization that had taken my brother from me at such a young age, but I couldn't help but wonder if I was missing some vital information. After all, I'd only been part of this world for less than 24 hours.

"If MOME is so unpopular, how are they still in charge?" I asked the room at large.

"They resort to blackmail a lot," Sol said. "And it's not as though they're elected and can be voted out. They're huge, they act like they're in charge everywhere, and… woe betide the people who don't acknowledge their jurisdiction."

"But if they're really that blatantly evil, surely people would just rise up against them," I countered. "They can't outnumber the entire magical population can they?"

"Well, they have a surprisingly good PR branch. They spin their misdeeds in ways that most people buy into. And besides, the average magic user doesn't run afoul of MOME very often. It's people that MOME deems 'dangerous' that get their basic human rights violated left, right, and center. So, most people find it easy enough to tell themselves that MOME is there to protect them, and not question things. Add to that the fact that they actually *do* stop real criminals, as well as people they just don't think should exist, and it makes it difficult for most folks to believe that they aren't as benevolent as they claim. If you told the whole world tomorrow that your brother was abducted at the age of eight and sent to a research facility at the base of an Andean mountain, most people would be outraged for as long as it took them to find out that he's a Phoenix."

"But he couldn't even turn into a Phoenix when they took him!" I objected.

"That doesn't matter. MOME would play up the fact that they suspected he would turn into a restricted creature when he came of age, and ignore the fact that they were playing a genetic long shot to even think that was a possibility. Everyone's afraid of the restricted creatures; they don't know any better. MOME has gone out of its way to play up the possible dangers of shifters who can access some of the rarer creatures, for centuries."

"Ok. Fine. So MOME are a bunch of assholes and have been for a while. Were they ever not assholes?" I asked.

Sol shrugged. "Hard to know for sure. Revisionist history and all. They've been around for a very, very long time."

I sighed.

"Trev, do you feel up to talking about what happened to you? I mean… you know… not like ten years of catch-up right this second, but… maybe a highlight reel?" I tried to smile while I asked it, but I was too worried.

You don't have to talk about it if you don't want to, I silently offered, just in case.

It's fine. Most of it isn't too bad.

"They came. They took me. I conquered, much later, by outsmarting them with computers."

That reminded me so strongly of the Trev I'd grown up with that it made me laugh out loud.

"Seriously though, Vic. I have a strong hatred for MOME, not so much because they did anything terrible to me, besides steal me away from you guys, but mainly just because they took so *many* of us. They never let us spend too much time together, so it's hard to be sure of numbers, but there were easily a hundred of us in my age group alone. Spread out, there were probably closer to five hundred. Five hundred families destroyed. Five hundred children raised by strangers. It just... it never ceases to piss me off."

"How did you escape?" I asked.

Trev eyed Sol for a moment, as though weighing what he should say in front of her, but then shrugged and started talking.

"I suppose it will all be in my file the next time you go to work anyway," he said to Sol. Then addressing the rest of us he continued, "I hacked the system, set off a bunch of viruses that made it impossible for MOME to monitor what was going on, and crawled out a conveniently overbuilt ventilation shaft. Easy."

"Ha! Really? Could you seriously crawl through the ventilation system without collapsing whatever section you were in? I thought that only worked in movies!" I said, while Sol's eyebrows rose to her hairline and Seamus smiled warmly at my brother.

"It *shouldn't* work outside of a movie, but for some reason MOME built theirs strong enough to hold a grown man," Trev explained.

"That's weird," I replied.

"It's an emergency escape system," Sol said, surprising all of us. "They built the ventilation system that way so that if part of the mountain collapses and the main entrance is cut off, there's an alternate route out of there. Also, ventilation below ground is serious business. You don't want that getting cut off, or people will die, so it's a seriously robust system."

"That makes sense, I suppose," I conceded.

"What I want to know," Sol said, "is why, if you have the ability to shut down the entirety of MOME's security and monitoring systems, you didn't escape earlier?"

Trev's smile faded at that question.

"I could have left anytime in the past, oh… probably eight years, certainly the last five, but I didn't…" his voice trailed off as he looked at me and then quickly away. My heart twisted in pain as I considered what might have kept him from escaping.

"You thought they would hurt us?" I asked.

Trev nodded, and wiped at the corner of his eyes. "For a long time they insisted that they had access to you and could get to you anytime if I didn't do what they asked, or if I tried to escape. I believed them until I was finally able to hack the system well enough to find your file. Then I realized that they didn't actually know where you guys were. That was a huge relief, and it certainly made me more confident in my rule breaking and trouble making efforts, but…"

"Why didn't you come find us?" I asked, my heart breaking all over again for the things my brother had gone through in the past ten years.

"I didn't want to lead them to you, Vic! I had nowhere else to go. What would I have done when I'd gotten out of there? Lived on the streets? I wasn't brave enough for that. At least with MOME I had a roof over my head and food in my belly. But I knew I wouldn't be welcome anywhere in the magical world. What Sol said about the restricted creatures is true. If anyone found out I was a Phoenix I would be ostracized, or worse, and certainly whoever found out would report me to MOME and then I'd be right back where I started. I knew that I would have eventually become desperate and tracked you guys down, and… and I probably would have led MOME right to your front door."

I suppressed a quiet sob and nodded my head. He had a point, damn it.

"So, what changed?" I asked, when my voice was under my control once more.

"Whatever you did to tip MOME off to where you were," Trev said. "The files I had flagged popped up with a new last known location. Which meant that MOME already knew where you were, so I did too. If MOME knew where to find you, then I had no reason not to try to get to you first. But I guess I didn't make it."

We all stared at Sol, but she just shrugged.

"My department found you because of the report filed by the Flagstaff police department. MOME has a database of 'dangerous' individuals that it cross-checks with every police database in the world. I'd been assigned to your file months ago. Knowing a bit about your parents, and what had happened to Trevor, I decided you were likely to see my family's side of things, so I did everything I could to get my superior to send me after you instead of someone else in my department. My family is keen to recruit as much help as we can get, and I thought offering to help you rescue your brother would get you both on our side."

We were all silent for a long moment, while we contemplated what all of that meant. I still had a million questions for Trevor, but I didn't want to make him recount every detail of his entire existence for the last ten years right away. He'd made it clear he wanted to give as few details as possible.

"So now what do we do?" I asked, eventually.

"Now," said Trev, "we go rescue my friends."

REV?

Nothing.

Trev?

"Damn it." I slapped my hands against the slightly damp rock beneath me and bounced my head off the rock wall behind me. Thankfully, rather than the urine I had feared it would smell like, it just smelled like wet rock and a bit of mold.

Trev, it's fucking pitch black down here. I can't even see my own hands.

I was supposed to be able to reach Trev from here. We weren't sure what the effective range on our telepathy was, but we'd tested it up to a kilometer earlier, and he shouldn't have been anywhere near that far away.

Is the rock messing with us? I asked the void.

And then I snickered. *The Rock doesn't want you to talk to your brother. The Rock will crush you after gratuitously referring to himself in the third person!*

It was a shame Trev wasn't getting any of this, because I was hilarious. Well, Trev would have found it hilarious, anyway. We used to watch WWF reruns with our dad—Mom preferred MMA.

I wondered how the rest of the rescue mission was going, now that I was locked up in this dank bit of dungeon.

It had been harder than I'd expected for Trev to bring us all on board with the rescue plan. To my surprise, it had been Seamus, and not Sol, who had been the most difficult to convince. Considering how often Seamus seemed determined to 'rescue' me, whether I needed it or not, I figured he'd be all for having a chance to play hero. It had only taken Trev explaining how many young kids were still being picked up by MOME every year to convince Sol to join in on the rescue mission. Apparently, while she didn't seem overly worried about how people Trev's age were still held captive by MOME, she couldn't abide the thought that small children were still being abducted. Seamus, on the other hand, objected to the risk to all of us, and I couldn't help but notice and be annoyed at how often he looked at me while he listed the possible 'perils' of taking the offensive and entering MOME territory. I happily informed Seamus that he didn't have to go at all if he was worried about the supposed perils, and he'd seemed half-inclined to take me up on my offer, until Trev admitted that part of the reason he was hell-bent on staging a rescue was to release his 'girlfriend' from MOME's grasp. That had made me want to pepper him with questions and a light hail of sibling teasing, but I refrained, since we had more important issues to address. Suddenly, Seamus was all in favor of the rescue mission, a change in stance that completely mystified me, but which I didn't bother to question at the time. We had spent the next few hours planning the details of our mission.

I sighed, wishing there were enough light to see by. I wanted to confirm that my disguise was still in place.

In what I was coming to understand as "standard Gwen behavior," the woman had shown up just before we were within sight of MOME and insisted that everyone but Sol needed a disguise. She had then turned all of us into pale-skinned, blonde-haired, blue-eyed people. Or at least, that's what she'd done with Trevor and Seamus, so I had to assume it was what she'd done to me. All I could see of my own disguise was the pasty white skin she'd given me. I had to admit that if Seamus and Trevor were anything to go by, no one was going to recognize us from this little adventure, assuming our disguises lasted for the duration. How Gwen had even known where we were, or what we were up to, was still a mystery to me, but I won't pretend we didn't appreciate the disguises.

Of course, when I'd asked her how she'd created them, her reply had just reaffirmed my assumption that she was decidedly lacking in sanity.

"Vic, darling, a goddess can do whatever she wants."

Goddess, right. Sure… I mean, hey, who am I to judge? I just started turning into a snow leopard yesterday… maybe she *was* a goddess.

She sure seemed delusional though.

Trev, when we get back home I need to find some normal friends.

Why do you continue to talk to ssssomeone who isssss not ressssponding? replied a voice that was decidedly not Trevor's.

O H SHIT.

Ummm… hello? I'm sorry, I didn't think I was broadcasting this to everyone.

Could anyone else do this? I had honestly thought this was just a twin thing.

I doubt there issss anyone elsssse who can hear bessssidessss me, but that issss only becausssse no one elsssse issss here.

Well, that was weird. According to Sol, there were close to two thousand people in this facility, and a number of them were supposedly in these very dungeons.

I must have accidentally broadcast some of that thought, because the other voice replied again.

No one who matterssss. There wassss one before you, but he… left.

Well, that sounded ominous.

Have you been here long? I asked, unsure what else to say.

Not long by my people'ssss ssstandardsss, but much longer than I would like.

Well, that told me precisely nothing.

What are you in for? I asked, wondering if my tone would be conveyed properly via telepathy.

I killed a handful of MOME agentsss who went where they should not have, the voice replied, in a tone that suggested that this was the obvious and rational response to such a scenario. *And you?*

Um… I resisted arrest, I suppose. I doubted that whoever I was talking to was on MOME's side, especially considering why she was here, but I didn't think I should just go revealing our master plan to anyone who could communicate telepathically with me. Besides, if she had heard me when I didn't mean for her to, who knew who else could be listening in to our conversation?

You are unssssure? the voice asked.

It's complicated, I replied.

Either you ressssissssted arresssst or you did not.

Well, I guess that depends on your perspective. I don't think I resisted arrest. I didn't think anyone was even trying to arrest me, but tell that to the MOME agent who claims that she was arresting me and that I ran away from her and then fought her off when she tackled me to the ground. I didn't know she was trying to arrest me, I just thought she was some crazy woman attacking me. She claims *she shouted that I was under arrest and to hold still, but I never heard her.*

The story was a bit far-fetched, I had to admit, but it amused me, and I was bored, and what the hell else was I going to do down here?

So you both ressssisssssted arresssst and did not? the voice asked.

Yep. It was like Schrödinger's arrest. I was both under arrest and not. I chuckled to myself. It was actually a pretty poor Schrödinger analogy, but it still made me laugh.

Sssschrödinger?

Maybe she had been in here a *looong* time.

Schrödinger was a scientist. He's famous for devising a thought experiment to point out a problem that he saw with the Copenhagen interpretation of quantum mechanics. He said that if you have a cat in a box and you cannot see or hear it, the cat is both alive and dead until you open the box, and then it is only one or the other.

And that was an oversimplification of Schrödinger's paradox, but it was enough to explain most of the internet memes on the subject.

Interessssting, the voice said. *Sssso, you were both under arresssst and not under arresssst until sssssomeone elsssse looked at the sssssituation and decsssided.*

Yeah. More or less.

Like I said, it wasn't the best analogy for this scenario.

And the people here decssssided you were under arresssst.

So it would seem, I admitted.

Doessss that make you the living cat, or the dead cat? the voice asked.

Hmm… if we take the analogy to its full extent, I guess I'm the dead cat, if one is fond of cats, but I prefer to think of myself as the live cat.

That issss underssssstandable, the voice said.

I was about to make a joke about people who don't like cats, when the door to my cell burst into flames and showered me in fiery shards.

"**W**HAT THE FUCK, Trev!?" I said, brushing the cinders off of myself.

"Sorry. These doors tend to be soundproof, so yelling was pointless, and I tried to warn you to stand back, but it seemed like you couldn't hear me. The rock must be messing with our connection."

I snickered again.

"The Rock will layeth the smacketh down upon our telepathy!"

Trev laughed loudly, and I wrapped him in a hug. As disconcerting as it was to see him with pasty white skin, blonde hair, and blue eyes, he still felt exactly right.

"Thanks for showing up. Where to?" I asked.

"Down," he said, gesturing towards a dark stone corridor lined with flickering torches that angled gently towards the center of the earth. The hallway carried the same scent of moss and damp stone that permeated my small chamber, but with the added flavor of burning pitch.

"Well, that's not ominous," I said, repressing a shudder even as we started down the corridor. "What's with the thirteenth-century dungeon look?"

Trev shrugged.

"Probably original. MOME is pretty old, and why update the dungeon?"

"Isn't it a little sketchy that a modern governing body still *has* a dungeon?"

"Don't get me started," Trev grumbled.

I laughed, but dropped the subject anyway. Trev had made his distaste for MOME quite clear already. He'd done one full tirade about tyranny and the oppression of the magically different during the planning stage of this mission, and we probably needed to focus on the task at hand.

It took much longer than I expected before we reached the next large wooden door in the corridor. I was mainly surprised by just how much solid rock separated each tiny six-foot by six-foot chamber.

Then I was extra surprised when Trev just grabbed the locked metal bolt that secured said door and held the assembly in his hand until it melted.

The door began a slow swing open, and Trev shouted, "Happy Hunting!" before we both booked it farther down the decidedly downward-sloping hall.

"What the hell, Trev?!" I asked, as we hurried farther down into the dungeon.

"What? That was a selkie. She'll have a grand time finding MOME agents and delivering a bit of payback."

"No. I mean the door! What's up with just melting the bolt off? Why did you have to explode mine into a bajillion pieces and shower me with its flaming ruins if you could just melt the bolt?"

"Oh, that. Your door was reinforced with a few spells I didn't recognize. Blowing it up was the best I could come up with on short notice. What did you do to piss them off, by the way?"

"Well, I didn't think it would be convincing if I went down without a fight. You should have seen the giant troll thing they set on me when they found me snooping around Sol's department. It was the size of an elephant."

"Probably Niko," Trev suggested. "Is he ok?"

"Who knows? He probably has a wicked headache. How prone are trolls to concussions?"

"Not very."

"Then he's probably fine. Friend of yours?" I asked.

"Kind of. Certainly not a bad guy. Trolls tend to get roped into doing MOME's dirty work pretty easily. The alternatives that MOME offers aren't terribly pleasant, so I can't blame them, really."

"Fair enough. Well, I tried to avoid permanent damage, but it didn't seem like he was extending me the same courtesy, so I'm not sure how concerned I am, in all honesty."

"Did you find what you were looking for, at least?" Trev asked, clearly ready to change the subject.

I nodded. "Yep. Just where you said it would be. Didn't have time to look at it before handing it off, though."

"Guess we'll have to trust Sol at some point," Trev said.

"True enough. If she were going to screw us over, she probably would've done it by now."

We finally reached another wooden door, and Trev did the same handle-melting trick as before.

"Seriously? What kind of mega-criminal do they think I am?" I asked, when the door popped open as soon as the bolt and handle disappeared.

Trev smiled.

"Trolls aren't easy to subdue," was all he said, before we turned and headed farther into the mountain.

"Dude, how many of these are we going to open? I didn't think they were going to be this far apart."

"My intel shows that the next one is the last occupied room in this part of the dungeon. One more selkie. That last one was a fire sprite."

I took a deep breath. Forty-eight hours ago, I had thought that magic was just something I enjoyed reading about on the weekends. The idea that we were releasing fire sprites and selkies from imprisonment, or that I had fought a troll earlier… it was still a bit much. I took a long look at Trev and suddenly felt a strange pang of longing.

"What's that look for?" he asked, even as we both kept up a light jog down the corridor.

"Just… none of this is new to you. I mean, Mom and Dad never told us about this stuff when we were little and then you were gone, my memory was wiped, and… I feel like a total outsider in this world, but you're sitting there smirking about how your sister brought down a troll, because you know about things like that."

"I'm not sitting, thank you very much, my legs are moving just as fast as yours."

"You *know* what I mean, Trev. This is your world. You fit in here."

Trev grabbed both my shoulders and pulled us both to a stop.

"Vic, you fit in here just as much as I do, you're just not used to it yet. The strangeness will fade pretty quickly, just wait, and… besides, I'm not really sure you get to complain about being the one who *wasn't* kidnapped and separated from your family for ten years."

I smacked my forehead against his shoulder, and then did it again for good measure.

"I'm so sorry, Trev. Of course I don't. What the fuck is wrong with me? I just… I guess I just haven't felt like myself in a long while and you seem pretty… together."

Trev wrapped me in a firm hug and when I felt his shoulders shake slightly, I looked up to catch his gaze.

Nope. Definitely not together. Trev's eyes were closed, but his breath was shaky and there was definitely moisture pooling at the corners of his eyes. I hugged him back even more fiercely than he'd hugged me.

"I'm sorry, Trev. Pity party over. I love you. I missed you. And I'm here for you any time you need to talk about it."

He smiled, stepping back, and we held hands as we started up our jog again.

The final door was just as easily dispatched as the others.

We were just about to turn around and follow the final selkie (a glorious, blue-skinned, green-haired, nymph-like creature whose webbed fingers and toes were visible in the fashionable jeans, tank-top, and flip-flop ensemble she was sporting) when a voice brought us to a standstill.

And what of me, Living Cat?

I turned and looked at Trev, who appeared so startled that I could only assume he'd heard it too.

"She's down here?" he muttered, taking me from zero to confused in no time flat.

"Do you know… her?"

"I didn't know she was in this part of the dungeon. She said… damn it!"

"What is it, Trev?"

"Come on, Vic. We can't leave her here."

"Do we have time to—"

Trev grabbed my hand and started sprinting down the corridor before I could finish speaking, leading us deeper into the mountain once more, this time at full speed.

O F COURSE THERE was another troll guarding this door.

Of course there was.

We had raced past another ten doors like the one that I had been locked behind after releasing the last selkie, but they had all been empty, according to Trev. Now, we reached one that was clearly occupied, even though Trev's reconnaissance had told him otherwise. Either that, or the giant creature that looked more like a swift-moving boulder was just here for his smoke break.

As we neared the door, I shifted to a fighting stance, getting ready to take this troll by surprise. I hoped I could cause enough of a distraction to give Trev time to pull whatever door trick was needed to get to whoever it was we were rescuing.

I was so focused on the rock-like behemoth before me that I almost didn't notice the tiny winged creature that launched itself from his shoulder until it was too late.

That was probably how she got most of her opponents.

Luckily, I saw the brief glint of steel in torchlight out of the corner of my eye just before she reached me, and I shifted to snow leopard just in time to send the tiny, sparkly, winged whatever-she-was flying past my head. If I was going to distract two opponents, especially ones as complementary as a troll and a pixie, for any length of time, I needed maximum reaction speed, and my human self had nothin' on my snow leopard.

Do not hurt them, Living Cat, they are only here under duresssss.

Well, *shit.*

That would have been more helpful to know before I'd provoked the flying warrior into trying to stab my eyes out, because now that she was at it, she was going to be rather difficult to discourage without doing some damage.

The pixie issss more ressssilient than the troll, Living Cat.

Oops. I must be projecting again. I *really* needed to work on that. I also needed to look into how many people could pick up on those projected thoughts, but now was not the time to worry about that. Now was the time to lay the smack down on the fierce-ass tiny warrior who was getting far too close to spearing my head with her six-inch sword for my liking.

The tricky thing was that I was batting her out of the air (or trying to) all while weaving in and out of the troll's legs, in order to make it as difficult as possible for the troll to grab me. The troll was delightfully slow, but if he (curious how I know it was a he? Go ahead, ask! I dare you. No? I'll give you a hint: I wouldn't have known if I hadn't been dancing between his legs looking up occasionally to keep tabs on a damnably fast pixie—and I would've been quite happy to live out my life with the mystery unsolved, let me tell you) grabbed me I was going to be one squished kitty.

The flying warrior dove at me again, at the same time that the troll shifted his weight to try to step on me, and I barely slipped between them without losing an ear. I hissed in frustration while turning around as quickly as I could to resume the fight, and was delighted to find that the winged fighter woman had embedded her tiny sword into the troll's skin and couldn't seem to dislodge it.

I roared in triumph, but before I could leap forward to make a pixie tattoo on the troll's leg, Trev let out his own whoop of victory, and I saw him slip inside the room beyond.

A moment later, he emerged from the dungeon cell with the most startlingly beautiful woman I'd ever seen. Her skin and hair were the color of midnight, covered in a faint iridescent sheen, and her irises were bright yellow, with slitted pupils like a snake's.

"Do not attack the Living Cat, Ssssylvesssstra. She meanssss you no harm."

It was odd to hear that voice coming from the woman standing before me instead of inside my head, but when tallied up with everything else that had happened to me this week, it really didn't rank very high on the Bizarre-O-Meter.

"Vic, this is Rhelia. Rhelia, this is my sister Victoria. We need to go before anyone realizes what we're up to. Especially now."

"Why especially now?" I asked, after shifting back to human.

"Because of Rhelia," he replied, as though that explained everything.

But Trev wasn't joking about being in a hurry. He turned and started sprinting up the corridor, Rhelia following close on his heels for a moment before she did… *something* that sped her past Trev and out of my line of sight. Having resumed my human shape, I started wrestling with my jeans so that I could follow them as soon as possible.

"Well, that was rude," came a voice from behind me.

I turned and saw the small winged warrior holding her sword over her small armor-plated shoulder and tapping one foot on the shoulder of the troll.

"Sorry," I said, as I pulled my sports bra and shirt back into place. "We have a whole escape plan thing we have to keep up with. If you guys need a distraction to get out of here, now might be a good time."

It surprised me that the troll and the winged fighter had listened to Rhelia at all, but I wasn't about to look a gift… whatever Rhelia was, she didn't seem much like a horse… in the mouth.

"I'd better catch up to them," I said, tugging my boots on, thankful that they were zip-ups instead of lace-ups, and then turning on my heel and taking off before they could rethink our truce.

By the time I caught up with Trevor, we were back in the standard institutional halls of the upper levels of MOME and Rhelia was nowhere in sight. I was about to ask him where she'd disappeared to, when all of a sudden he was no longer running beside me.

Instead he was lying on the floor a few yards ahead of me, scrambling to fight off a crazed, sparkle-fanged moron.

"**E**DIK!! GET OFF of him, you lunatic!" I shouted, launching myself into the fray.

Edik was clearly doing his best to rip Trev's throat out, so I didn't waste time trying to be nice. I kicked him in the head as soon as an opportunity presented itself, and then, as the inevitable shock of my boot hitting his face sent him reeling backwards, launched myself at his shoulders so that I would be between him and Trev.

"Victoria, darling, I do not like this disguise. Where are your beautiful eyes? Who is this pale whisper of a woman?"

I was a little surprised that Edik didn't prefer the blonde that Gwen had turned me into, since that seemed more like his type, but I honestly cared so little about what he found attractive that I skipped right past his comment and continued punching him in the face.

"Ow! Why did you do that, beloved?"

"Edik, seriously. I don't know what you're doing here, but if you ever touch my brother again, I will kill you."

"Brother?" he asked, finally letting his head fall back to the floor.

"Yes. My brother. Not that it's any of your damned business who he is."

As Edik was now lying down and cradling his likely broken nose, I got off of him and stood up.

"If you ever attack me or anyone I care about again, Edik, I swear it will be one of the last things you do. Now, what the hells are you doing here?" I asked.

Edik stared at me with such a strange look in his eyes that for a moment I wondered if he was concussed.

"You can't charm her, vamp, so stop wasting your time," Trevor said from beside me.

"I'm here because I love you. We're meant to be, Victoria, you will come to see it in ti—"

Edik's voice cut off as I wrapped my hand around his throat, picked him up off the ground, and slammed him against the wall. I made a mental note to be shocked later about how I was suddenly strong enough to use only one hand to pin a two hundred pound person to the wall, but for now I just clamped down on his throat with my hand and growled threateningly.

"Let's try this again," I gritted out, so *very* sick of Edik's shit. "Why are you here? And don't pretend it has anything to do with me, asswipe. You may be a moron with no sense of personal space, but you didn't follow me to a MOME facility in the Andes just to profess your misguided amorous feelings for me."

Edik shrugged, after a moment, and then wrenched his way out of my grip.

"Fine. You're right. I suppose I shouldn't have expected you to buy the besotted lover ruse for much longer.... I'm looking for my daughter."

I FELT MY brain scratch like dirty vinyl, but Edik just kept talking.

"I heard you talking about MOME in your home, and then that Gwen person showed up and I decided to hitch a ride."

That had to have been the truth, because it didn't make any damned sense as a lie.

"Daughter? Wait, what? How do vampires even work in this world? And how could you have hitched a ride? We'd have seen you. And how could you have known where Gwen was taking us? We didn't even know!"

"I didn't know where she was taking you, but I was desperate to follow you to MOME, and I had to hope she would get you closer than I could have gotten on my own. And as for you not seeing me there, I am quite capable of shadow walking, thank you very much."

I opened my mouth to ask a hundred more questions, but Trev cut me off.

"We'll do vampire 101 later, Vic. We have to go. Now."

I wanted to argue with that, because nothing that Edik had just said made any sense. Like why he had thought I could lead him to MOME when I hadn't even known MOME existed until a day ago, and he'd been stalking me for three days. But Trev had a point—we were low on time. Besides, that was when we heard a bunch of incoherent screaming from the hallway ahead of us, and Edik jumped up and ran in the opposite direction.

Since we didn't wish to confront the screaming ourselves, we followed him.

I could hear cursing in at least three languages behind us, as well as what sounded like chanting. I might have been new to the whole "magic is real" thing, and no, I wasn't super clear on how everything worked yet, but I certainly wasn't new to the *idea* of magic. And any experienced fantasy nerd, whether gamer, reader, or movie goer, knows that bad guys chanting in languages you don't speak and running in your direction means shit is about to go *down*.

We quickly picked up speed, right on Edik's heels, as we transitioned from vampire-smack-down to runneth-the-hell-away. I didn't have a Holy Hand Grenade of Antioch shoved in my back pocket, and whatever was behind us was definitely in possession of some big, pointy teeth—metaphorically, at least.

We plowed through a few identically bland institutional hallways, turning seemingly at random, but presumably following some sort of pattern that Edik could sense. At any rate, Trev never suggested that we follow a different course, so I just went along with it. Each hallway was the same disgusting off-white lit with flickering halogen lights. I had no idea how anyone kept their bearings in a place like this. I generally had an excellent sense of direction, but I couldn't keep track of where we were in this MOME facility. Perhaps it was because we were too far beneath the mountain, or perhaps it was simply because every damned hallway looked exactly the same.

Then we turned a hard right into a fifteen-by-fifteen foot room, painted in the same disgusting eggshell and lit with the same shitty halogen bulbs as every hallway we'd just gone through, and I was so surprised that I actually ran into Edik's back.

"The fuck?" I asked, finally looking up as I bounced off of Edik's frame, almost knocking both of us to the floor.

"Well, that's a surprise," I heard Trevor mutter behind me, and then I stepped around Edik to see the rest of the room.

I ignored the bland trappings of the place as my eyes were instantly drawn to the two women standing in the center of it. Namely Gwen and someone I'd never met who had mouse-brown hair, brown eyes, and skin that looked like it had never seen the sun.

THE PALE WOMAN looked nonplussed to see all of us there, but it wasn't until I heard Edik scream something incomprehensible in what I thought might have been Russian that the other woman paled a bit. Then she smiled weakly, as though she thought she could smooth things over with the right facial expression.

Edik, however, looked furious. Oddly, despite the number of times I had broken his nose, or otherwise beaten the crap out of him, I had never seen him look angry. It wasn't a good look on him. Too much sneering—facial features all distorted—it ruined the symmetry of his near perfect face. Made him look like the douchetart he actually was.

"WHERE IS MY DAUGHTER?!"

Huh. The plot thickens. I couldn't help but share the thought with Trevor, and he shared a sensation of humor with me, on top of his general annoyance at being held up in our escape. I, for one, was curious how the new person that Gwen was talking to was involved in this latest development.

"I don't know," said the pale brunette who had been talking to Gwen moments earlier. "They took her."

"*They* took her? *THEY* took her!? YOU took her from me!"

"I did not. We left together. Voluntarily. To be with Guille, but he…"

The brunette looked embarrassed.

"B! She's not an adult yet. You can't take her out of the country without my consent, no matter who you've chosen to run away with. You should have left her with me."

"She didn't want me to leave her behind."

"Then you should have stayed."

If flames could have shot out of Edik's eyes I imagine they would have, but luckily that didn't seem to be on his list of skills. By this point, Trev was cursing almost silently behind me. I was waiting for him to suggest that we keep moving and leave Edik to his fate, but it hadn't happened yet. In the meantime, I will admit to being damned curious about what was going to happen next.

B shrugged.

"We were both bored. It's not as though there's anything much to do in that town, and you were so hell bent on keeping us hidden from the rest of the vampires that we felt like shut-ins."

"And tell me, dear B, what happened to you as soon as you made yourselves known to the magical community outside of our family?"

B looked entirely sheepish.

"Well, I won't pretend I'm not disappointed about how things turned out with Guille, but—"

"But WHAT? You're trapped here at MOME, aren't you? This is their primary research center. Did you *know* that? Did you know anything about that asshole before you ran off and handed over our DAUGHTER to him?"

I wasn't a fan of Edik at all, and I thought the yelling was stupidly over the top, but for just a moment I felt sorry for him. The context was clear enough, and while I certainly couldn't blame anyone who wanted to get as far away from Edik as humanly (or vampirely) possibly, the whole stealing away with his kid who winds up in MOME's hands struck me as pretty damned heartbreaking. Then I remembered what Edik was like, and the heartbreak ended.

"I didn't know he worked for MOME. Thanks to you practically keeping us in a damned cage, I barely understood what MOME was! If you had let us talk to *anyone* else I might have known what the risks were. Instead you tried to keep us wrapped in fucking bubble wrap and we had no idea what we were getting ourselves into!"

Yeah. There we go. I should have realized before I even started to feel bad for him that he was likely the bringer of his own destruction.

"It never even occurred to you that people might have a more than healthy fascination with a Dhampir!?"

That was a fair point. Dhampir, huh? I wondered if that word carried any of the meaning it held in certain works of fiction.

Gwen raised a hand and spoke before either of them could continue.

"There are approximately twenty guards headed this way at the moment. The only reason they aren't here yet is thanks to some handy spellwork Trevor left behind for them in one of the hallways, and I don't think now is the best time for the rest of this conversation. B," she said, turning towards the young female vampire, "when was the last time you saw Renata?"

"Guille said he was going to take her for a hike two days ago. They never came back. It took me a day to track them here. I spent the morning sneaking through this place."

Gwen looked impressed.

"They didn't catch you until an hour ago?"

"They didn't catch me at all!" B replied angrily. "I walked into this room and accidentally let the door latch behind me. I couldn't get out again."

"What made you come in here?" Edik asked, looking around himself for the first time.

I had to admit I hadn't paid much attention to the room, aside from the lame paint job, until Edik raised the question, but just as I started to take in the details of the various apparati around the room, and the creepy metal table in the center of it, Trev jumped up on the table, pushed one of the ceiling panels out of the way, and started crawling into one of the vents.

"Where are we headed, exactly?" I asked, climbing up on the table and pulling myself up into the vent behind him, following his feet as they disappeared down the large metal shaft.

"We're headed to the northern slope," he replied. "The ventilation system ends in the middle of a cliff face, so they don't leave much security on it."

I wondered if Edik and B would follow us, or if they had their own way of dealing with the security here. I knew Gwen would just do whatever the fuck suited her fancy.

"Right. Makes sense," I said, taking a deep breath. We were already in the shafts that led to our exit point? I enjoyed a brief moment of feeling hopeful that we were going to get out of here without anyone dying.

Of course, that was when the alarms started going off.

~~~

"And what does this mean, exactly?" I asked Trevor, as we both sped up our snakelike movements along the ventilation shafts.

"It means," said Trev, as he deftly "vaulted" over another of the down shafts that we ran into periodically, which we had to clear by shimmying as close to the edge of one side as we could get and then stretching our arms across and pulling/pushing the rest of our bodies across the gap without sliding into it, "that they finally noticed that we freed up the entire high-security roster."

I nodded, ignoring the fact that he couldn't see me.

"And that's a good thing?" I asked.

"We need the distraction."

"Right. And what about the two vampires and er... Gwen?"
~~~

"Your redheaded friend smells like a deity of some kind, so she likely can't be trapped, the vampire who followed you seemed like the kind of asshat we wouldn't mind seeing interrogated by MOME's goons, and as for B and her daughter… could be risky, but they can probably take care of themselves."

"Even her daughter?" I asked.

"No one likes a Dhampir, but she can very likely take care of herself."

"She's a kid, Trev."

He swiveled his head around and stared at me until I realized the ridiculousness of what I was saying. For all I knew, she was our age. Certainly she was likely to be only a few years younger, and if…

"Are Dhampirs the badasses everyone writes them to be in Urban Fantasy books?"

Trevor chuckled.

"Very much Dorina Bassarab style, from the few I've met, though perhaps slightly less… intense."

I chuckled at that. Then frowned, when I realized why he'd likely met any Dhampirs at all, let alone a few, since they were supposed to be incredibly uncommon.

"Does MOME kidnap *all* of them?" I asked.

"The ones they can get to before the vampires kill them, yes."

"For 'research' purposes?"

"Yep. And to 'protect the people,' don't forget that. Same as me, I guess. Although, to be fair, the vampires do try to kill them all, so MOME is providing some protection in the case of Dhampirs."

I scowled at Trev's back but said nothing.

As we'd been talking, we'd turned at one of the intersections and started scurrying slightly uphill.

"Sol and Seamus should be up here somewhere, if everything went the way it was supposed to," Trevor said, as we reached another intersection.

"Well, since everything else has gone so swimmingly, I don't see how they could have run into trouble," I replied, with just a *hint* of sarcasm.

Trevor chuckled, ahead of me, and I decided to stop talking and focus on where I was crawling. I was impressed that he had the whole place mapped out well enough in his head to keep track of where we were and where we needed to be. I still knew where we were pointed in terms of cardinal directions, thanks to whatever directional sense my snow leopard form granted me, but I was lost in terms of these tunnels of ventilation shafts and hallways that all seemed identical and veered off arbitrarily.

I was still contemplating whether someone in charge of MOME might be a wererabbit trying to make this research facility feel like home when Trev stopped abruptly ahead of me.

"I think we found them." His voice sounded… less than optimistic.

"Is that not a good thing?" I asked.

"Not when they've got five high-security mages for company," he replied.

"Does that mean we're fighting our way out?"

"Depends on whether or not you want your friends back."

I smiled. I hadn't had a good fight in… well, not since I left my old dojo, and even that had just been sparring, not a real test of my skills.

"I could use some exercise," I said, to the back of Trevor's head. When he said nothing in response, I added, "I don't have many friends Trev, it'd be a shame to lose these ones."

That seemed to convince him.

"You may want to shift," he said, just before the floor fell out from under us.

I WAS ALL for having the element of surprise, but I generally would have preferred to not be getting surprised right along with my target. Things must have been about to get hairy though, because Trevor went down flaming.

Of course, Trev, who could blink and become an eight-foot-wing-spanned fire bird, didn't think anything of the drop from the ventilation shaft. Whereas I had to do my best to roll through a fall that left me crashing into the linoleum floor eight feet below where we'd started.

Yeah, sure, Trevor had warned me to shift, but I couldn't call on it quite that fast yet, and I didn't know if I was better off in cat form anyway. After all, I had trained for my san-dan in Shotokan as a human, not as a snow leopard.

In the beginning, not shifting seemed like the right decision. The mages who were in that room with Sol and Seamus all started screeching (presumably slinging spells) as soon as the flaming ball of wings and fury that was my brother descended into the room, and they all seemed inclined to take my human-looking female frame for granted. In our planning stages, Sol had mentioned more than once that mages weren't very good at detecting weres, so I supposed now was my chance to take advantage of their ignorance about my powers. The nearest one didn't even throw any spells at me, simply stepping forward with a pair of handcuffs— presumably magic ones, but I never let him get close enough to find out.

I ducked under the arm he swung out to grab me, a horribly telegraphed move that would have ended up with him unconscious at my feet if I hadn't been defending against multiple opponents, and swept my leg out to take his feet from under him while also dodging something sparkly that flew from the hands of the next closest mage.

So, some forms of magic were visible. Useful intel. In the meantime, it also helped that mages, or at least *these* mages, telegraphed their spellcasting like crazy. Maybe they couldn't help it, maybe there was no way to cast without the wild hand gestures and targeted glaring accompanying each spell. I was too new to all of this to know what the rules for mages were, but as it was, I had multiple seconds of warning before each attack came, which was *more* than enough.

The second mage closest to me was still casting her next spell when I punched her in the gut. I would have aimed for somewhere more permanently damaging, but I wasn't sure what the deal with all of these MOME people was. How many of them thought they were doing good in the world? How many of them were there to take things down from the inside like Sol was? How many of them actually thought it was ok to abduct young children for 'research' purposes and keep them from their families?

Whatever the answer was, either Trev already had it, or he just didn't care. The mage who was fighting Seamus—who had shifted to his wolf form and was happily digging teeth and claws into said mage—was reaching into his leather vest (I hadn't noticed until that moment, but three out of five of the mages were dressed like they'd driven Harleys to get here) when he suddenly burst into flames with a bloodcurdling shriek. I caught sight of Trevor's wing clipping him just before he ignited, and wondered what on earth he'd been about to reach for that made my brother decide he deserved a flaming death.

I didn't have time to ask, though, as that bit of pyrotechnics set the remaining mages, who *weren't* engulfed in flames, scrambling to regroup. I decided the safest thing was to render unconscious the one I'd just hit in the gut. I clipped her just under her jaw and watched her collapse.

Just as I was about to attack the mage who had come after me with handcuffs earlier, I felt something hot graze my back and shoulder, and ducked just as something sizzled past my ear. I could smell my hair burning where the spell had grazed me.

A heartbeat later, searing pain jolted through me, as my nerves finally registered whatever had been done to my back and shoulder by the spell.

Some instinct made me reach for my snow leopard form before I could even think twice about it. The pain was gone as soon as I shifted, and I wondered if that was because I was no longer attached to the body that had been hurt, or some other, more mystical reason. I didn't have time to contemplate it for long though, as more spells were slung around me.

And now I realized why Trev had suggested I shift before we'd even hit the floor in this room.

While I had been able to see some of the spells being slung in my human form, as a snow leopard it looked like I could see… well, everything. All magic seemed to be visible to me. Not only could I see even more spells whizzing through the air, as my friends did their best to dodge them and take down the mages, I could also see a thin skin of power around the mages who remained conscious. I could even see residual magic along surfaces throughout the room where spells had either hit and bounced off, or passed right through the materials. It was an interesting view.

In addition, my other senses, smell and sound, as well as the vibrations picked up by my whiskers, were so heightened in this form that I found myself reacting to things I would never have noticed as a human. And my muscles… they responded to my call so quickly that I almost felt as though time was slower as a snow leopard. Maybe it was.

I saw Sol take down the mage who had cast whatever spell had burned me, and I almost felt sorry for the bastard as she tore into his arm with her teeth. She was in her gloriously huge panther form, and I was once more impressed with the deep black of her fur and the bright yellow of her eyes. It looked as though she, at least, had decided not to kill our opponents, as she released the mage's arm once he appeared to have passed out from either shock or blood loss.

He was the last to go down. Five for five.

Trev reappeared as a human. He seemed untroubled by the fact that he was naked.

"Don't anyone else bother to shift, unless you have something of dire importance to add. We need to get out of here, quickly. Follow Vic and me through this ventilation shaft now. If we can get to the exit before they realize we're using the vents, we might just make it out before they try to drug us, or worse."

Then he turned into a flaming bird once more, shooting up through the gaping hole that we had crashed through earlier. I didn't hesitate, but leapt through the hole and reveled in how powerful my snow leopard body was. I didn't know if a normal snow leopard could have made that leap—I'd have to do some research on that front—but either because I was a shifter, or because snow leopards were badass, the eight feet between floor and ceiling felt like nothing to me.

Being a snow leopard was so awesome.

L ESS THAN A quarter of an hour later, I saw Trev disappear suddenly from in front of me and felt a cold wind slap me in the face as I neared the open vent that waited ahead. The drop beneath me was shear; climbable, certainly, but far enough down that I wasn't stoked about the idea of scaling it without a rope. Since I didn't see Trev below me, I looked up. There he flapped lazily, a firebird relaxing on a heady breeze. Assuming we were in for a long, upwards climb, I shifted to my human form.

Come on up!

Even though we'd been doing it since Trev had shown up at the house in Flagstaff, it still blew my mind that we could communicate telepathically.

I still can't believe this works! Our five-year-old selves would be so stoked, I thought.

They may have encouraged me to… practice here, Trevor said. That made my mouth go dry. What else had they forced him to do?

Trev, if it's… we don't have to use it. We can just wait till we've both shifted to human again and talk then.

It's fine, Vic. This part was never so bad, and it always made me think of you. Once I started getting it right I got really excited about showing off for you once I found you again.

That made me smile. Typical Trevor, really. Must share all new discoveries with Vic, otherwise they don't count.

You never gave up on us, did you?

Before Trevor could respond, a hand was resting on my back and pushing me forcefully towards the opening.

"Now, now, now. Must go now. No time to hesitate. Go. Go. GO!"

The last go was followed by a shove so firm that I catapulted to the edge of the vent and would have free fallen the 1000 feet to my rocky death below if I hadn't managed to catch the lip of metal that had formerly kept the grate in place.

"Sol! What the—"

The "fuck" died on my tongue as I turned to see a terrifying green cloud of… I didn't want to know what, that was seething behind Seamus' and Sol's fast-moving, now-human forms.

The green cloud was so horrifying that I didn't even notice that Sol and Seamus were both naked, let alone take a moment to appreciate the view, as they burst out of the vent and onto the cliff wall, just barely catching the rock in time to prevent themselves from plummeting to the ground below. Instead, I just angled myself so that I could reach the rock face above and to the left of the hole I'd almost fallen out of and started scrambling for holds as fast as I could.

There are some benefits to growing up in the Rockies. One of them is having access to world-class climbing every weekend throughout one's entire childhood. I was never going to be a professional climber—I spent too much of my time training in martial arts for one thing—but I loved to climb, and could get up and down your average cliff face with minimal trouble. At the moment I was doing my best to "sprint" up the face before me. I don't know if it was some sixth sense provided by being a were, or if it was just a basic human instinct, but something told me that whatever the festering cloud of green slime that was chasing Seamus touched would not come out unscathed, or even recognizable.

Luckily, Sol and Seamus seemed comfortable enough on the rock face we had suddenly all found ourselves scaling, though they were probably highly motivated by the cloud of roiling death that seemed to be dissipating into the clear void beneath us. Still, neither of them seemed paralyzed by a fear of heights, or so unsure of their next move that they couldn't keep going. They were both seeking holds and making use of them with the seasoned motions of people who had done this before.

Thank the gods. This was going to be a long enough climb as it was, we didn't need to add stressed out newbs to the equation.

"What in the hells *was* that thing?" I asked Sol, as we picked our way up the cliff face that towered above us. There wasn't as much left above us as there had been below, but it was still a formidable wall. Thankfully, it was made of a friendly granite composite that had eroded into some relatively positive holds. Of course, the downside of these types of walls is that they crumble easily, but we weren't going to think about that just now. We were just going to climb… and worry about the creepy cloud of whatever-it-was behind us.

"*That*," Sol explained, as she sought out her next handholds, gingerly testing their solidity before putting her full weight on them, "was a spell that is supposed to be banned. A fucking scrambler that supposedly only the 'bad guys' use. If it touches you… let's just say it turns you into a Picasso, and not in a good way."

"So… we have your MOME buddies to thank for having one tailing us?"

Sol grunted.

"Buddies isn't the word I would choose, but yeah. Three of the five mages we were up against in that room are known for using illegal spells. They are *supposedly* only sent after the most dangerous criminals in the magical world, but…"

"But they sent them after us?"

"Well, first they sent them to 'help' with my interrogation of Seamus. Once they heard me ask him about *you*, they decided I needed backup. When they decided I wasn't being rough enough with Seamus, that's when everything went to hell in a handbasket."

"Ah. So we showed up just in time, then," I muttered. "Shit!" I added, when one of my handholds broke off and tumbled away from me. "Rock!" I cried, even though there was no one below me. Well, no one that I cared about, anyway. Seamus and Sol were both climbing to my right, not far enough beneath me to be in line of any rockfall I might create, and Sol had basically caught up already.

"Yeah, well, I could probably have gotten us out of there," she said. "But not without completely blowing my cover. As it stands now… HQ will probably forgive me for not wanting my captive beat to shit, and then you and Trevor clearly showed up to break Seamus free, and I merely followed you."

"What about the guy you tore up back there?"

"I can write that off as protecting Seamus. Technically, there are laws protecting captives, even MOME captives. It would be very by the book of me to have defended him."

"And will they—shit!"

Another hold crumbled out of my hand, and I was left hanging by my left arm. I had been testing holds before I took them, but some seemed more solid than they actually were. I made a point of not looking down at the over 1000 foot drop below me.

"It's only a matter of time before one of us loses our grip completely," Sol said.

I looked at her and Seamus, both still climbing along steadily. Seamus hadn't said a word since we'd started our ascent. He might have been shitting his pants (figuratively that is) but it was hard to tell. Trev had flown up ahead of us, and I wondered if he was doing general reconnaissance, or had already seen something that concerned him.

Then I remembered that I could ask him.

How's it looking up there, Trev?

For a long moment there was no reply. Then, suddenly—

Fuck, fuck, fuck, fuck, fuck! Must fly faster. Vic! Change direction. Now!

What? Trev, it's over 1000 feet to the bottom an—

NOW, Vic! Go, go, go!

"Shit! Downclimb! Now! Trev sounds scared shitless and is telling us to reverse course."

No one argued, though I could tell they didn't like the idea any more than I did.

Downclimbing was always sketchier than going up, especially on a face like this one where anything could crumble out from under you. There was no way to check holds first when you were downclimbing, especially not when you were in a hurry to escape… whatever the hell had Trevor cursing like a Spanish sailor.

All three of us descended as quickly as we safely could, but apparently that wasn't fast enough. A ball of flames and wings shot past me, which I could only assume was Trev, and then there were blasts of magic shooting past me on all sides and Sol and Seamus were both releasing a string of curses as they went.

There was no way for us move faster without greatly increasing our likelihood of falling to our deaths, and there was no way to dodge the spells being slung at us easily either. The best we could do was try to move erratically, but that wasn't exactly easy when trying to scale a cliff in reverse.

"We're so screwed," I muttered, as another spell flew past my shoulder. "At least these mages seem to aim like storm troopers."

As soon as I said it, I felt the rock under my right foot tumble away at same moment that I had let go with my left hand to bring it to the next hold beneath me. I felt my left foot pull back from the rock, as my body swung wildly to the right, and then I began to scream as my right hand held, held, held, held for all it was worth, hundreds of hours of muscle memory doing their damnedest to save my life, and then I felt the rock there crumbling away too.

The fact that it was probably a spell loosening the rock around me, and not just shitty luck, didn't make much of a difference as I felt my body start the free fall that would end with it splattered all across the jagged boulders below me. Somehow, I suspected that turning into a snow leopard would only leave fuzzier remains spread out across the valley floor. My right shoulder bounced off of the cliff face as I tumbled into the air, knocking the wind out of me, and leaving my arm feeling numb at my side. I'd probably lost a fair chunk of flesh on that rock—naked climbing certainly had its added risks.

I heard Sol shout my name as I fell away from the cliff face, and Seamus let out a bloodcurdling cry as he leapt for my body. He crashed into me, already fully changed to wolf form by the time we smashed together, and I wondered what the hell good he thought he was doing. All he'd managed to do was push us both farther from the side of the cliff face, which I suppose was a good thing if one didn't want to die hitting every damned ledge on the way down, but it left a lot to be desired as far as saving our asses went. We were still going to die horribly when we hit the giant scree pile that was getting closer with every last beat of my frantic heart.

I wanted to thank him for trying, or curse him for throwing his life away with mine, but I couldn't do anything but scream. It wasn't a high-pitched keening or even a crying wail, it was just a sustained emptying of my lungs. Just me raging against the dying of the light.

Then, before the ground could swallow us in its rocky maw, something else hit me hard from the side. I barely managed to keep my grip on Seamus' furry form as everything turned black around us.

I BLINKED AND found myself standing in a small
forest clearing gazing stupidly at a tree that
looked a lot like a figure in a hooded robe,
holding a scythe. Seamus was still clutched in my
arms, breathing heavily in wolf form.

"What the —" I had been about to say hell, but
I stopped myself. Just in case.

"Where are we?" I asked the clearing at large.
This place was familiar. I suppose it had only been
a few days since my last camping trip, in the clearing where all of this started, but it already seemed
like a lifetime ago.

I looked at Seamus as I gently placed him on the
ground in front of me, but he just gave me a wolfy
shrug.

"Thanks, Seamus," I said, rubbing his head. "Are
we dead?" I wondered aloud. "I seriously hope
we're not dead."

YOU ARE NOT DEAD.

"Whoa… who is that?"

I AM THE TREE OF LIFE.

I focused my eyes on the lone oak tree in a glade full of scotch pines and felt a weird tingle go up my neck. It was the oak from the night that I had met Gwen. The one that looked suspiciously like a robed, hooded figure holding a scythe.

"Are you sure you're not Dea—"

I AM THE TREE OF LIFE. MY RESEM-BLANCE TO ANY PERSON OR CHARAC-TER, REAL OR IMAGINARY, IS PURELY CO-INCIDENTAL.

"Ok. Ok. Sheesh. You don't have to go all legal disclaimer on me. I get it. You are the Tree of Life. Fine. It's just that you look an awful lot like Terry Pratchett's Dea—"

LIFE. YES. THANK YOU. I APPRECIATE IT. I HAVE BEEN GROWING THESE BRAN-CHES TO LOOK MORE ALIVE FOR A VERY LONG TIME.

I shut up, not wanting to waste any more time arguing with the big tree with glowing eyes. Had they been glowing when we'd arrived? I didn't think they had been, but whatever, I had more im-portant matters to worry about at the moment. I started to stand up and pull my hand from Seamus' fur, but he whined and leaned hard against my leg, unwilling to put any space between us. I dug my hand back into his fur.

"So, Dea— er… Life! It's good to see you. I think…"

I looked around the clearing again.

"Did you just save us?"

The hooded tree figure that *definitely wasn't Death* shook its head.

I DO NOT SAVE PEOPLE.

"Right. Ok. Cool. You didn't save us. Do you know who did?"

ME.

"Umm… didn't you just say that you don't save people?"

GWEN HELPED. ACTUALLY, SHE DID THE SAVING, BUT SHE IS MY INSTRU-MENT.

"I'm not a damned violin, you talking tree."

The leather-clad redhead stood in the circle next to Death, and I couldn't help but wonder how much of this they had known about back on that first day in the woods. I mean, that's an awfully convenient setup otherwise. Still, first things first.

"Thank you," I said, meaning it. I really didn't want to die in general, but least of all smashed into a bunch of tiny pieces at the bottom of a mountain in the Andes. Well, ok, maybe not "least of all," I could think of far worse ways to go, really, but damn it. I had a lot to live for yet, and my long-term goals involved dying peacefully in my sleep in my hundreds, or at least dying splattered at the bottom of a cliff when I was a LOT older.

"I can't ever repay you," I said. "I really had no way out of that."

Gwen smiled, and the amount of tooth she bared made me start to sweat a bit.

"You *can* repay us, actually," she said, "now that you mention it."

"Oh?" I asked, feeling decidedly nervous. "How, exactly?"

"Don't look so frightened," she said. "I'm the goddess of good fortune and helping those who help themselves. I don't have any nefarious plans."

"You're the goddess of luck?" I asked. Honestly, if Sol and Trev hadn't independently confirmed that they thought she was a deity back in Bolivia, I doubt I would have believed she was anything more than the delusional woman who claimed to be my narrator.

"You can call me Serendipity if you like, but I prefer Guenhwyvar, and Gwen is easier on the tongue."

"Umm… does that make you a new god, or—?"

Gwen laughed, and suddenly her hair looked like it was liquid fire mixed with rubies, her eyes were molten emeralds, her skin glowed like radioactive gold, and everything about her was moving in its own private wind.

"One of the oldest, actually," she said, with a voice that sounded like seven different voices, each in a different octave, all speaking at once.

"Ok… dramatic effect taken. What can I do to help you that you can't already do yourself?" I asked.

"Well, I can't be everywhere at once, though I do try. There's just not enough belief these days to go around, and my powers aren't what they used to be."

I nodded again. Fair enough, omnipresence was probably a rough deal, really. I was going to have to interrogate someone about how *any* of the gods actually existed, ASAP, but I had a feeling this wasn't the right moment.

"So, I use agents," Gwen continued.

"Agents?"

"Agents of fortune," she replied. "Today, because I was already nearby, I was able to tackle you out of the sky and save you, but if I had been in say… Helsinki, for some reason, I might not have been able to get to you in time. As you can no doubt appreciate from very recent experience, seconds can make all the difference in some cases."

I nodded, not sure I liked where this was going, but unsure how it could be avoided.

"I need agents on the ground," she said. "I have some, spread around here and there, but it's difficult to find reliable people who can meet the demands of the job."

"And what are the demands of the job, precisely?" I asked.

"Pretty straightforward: whenever you see someone in need of help, who has been doing all they can to help themselves but just needs a bit of a nudge, you do whatever you can to help."

"What does that mean, they've been doing all they can to help themselves?"

Gwen shrugged.

"Means different things for different folks, I suppose. Mostly I just meant that they haven't given up. I'm not trying to constrain how you help people on your own time, you're welcome to help whoever you like if it's something you can do on your own, but what you do with the power I grant you… I'd like that only to be for those that meet my requirements."

"And am I only helping *people*?"

Gwen didn't answer, but shifted into a beautiful timber wolf, then an owl, then a snake, then a very uncomfortable-looking dolphin, then back to her two-legged form.

"I wasn't willed into being solely by humans. I help *all* of those who help themselves. Animals are generally first on my list, to be honest."

She took a good look at me and I shivered a bit, wondering what all she saw beyond the human who stood before her.

"Are you willing to assist me?" she asked.

"Dea—er… Life said you were his instrument. What did he mean by that?"

She laughed, looking over her shoulder at the shaped tree behind her, who merely gazed impassively out of two glowing eyes deeply recessed in the hood he'd formed out of his branches.

"Life and I go way back. We're two of the very first gods willed into being on this world…. He was technically around before I was, and some of my powers come from his. I wouldn't call myself his instrument any more than I would call the sun and tides his instruments, but you could say that he uses them when he feels the need."

I thought about that.

"So, Life, if I sign up to help Gwen, are you going to be calling on me all the time to help you out as well?"

It was difficult to tell, but I thought the figure might have shrugged.

I DO NOT NEED HUMANS RUNNING AROUND DOING MY BIDDING.

Well, if that was another answer along the lines of "I don't rescue people," it wasn't particularly re-assuring, but I decided not to worry about it for the moment. Another, darker thought occurred to me, requiring my immediate attention.

"If I say no, do we go right back to free falling to our deaths?" I asked.

Gwen's face paled.

"Holy shit, Vic. No! What do you take me for?"

I sighed and ran a hand through Seamus' coat for a moment. He hadn't reacted much since we'd arrived here. Certainly, he wasn't frantic, the way a real wolf would be after being thrown from a cliff and then whisked into a random bit of woods. Considering how frantic I felt, I was impressed at his calm.

"Sorry, I just… I dunno. Gods are supposed be tricksters."

"You've been reading too many fantasy books," Gwen replied.

I raised an eyebrow at her. "Oh yeah. Clearly that has been in no way useful at preparing me for my completely normal and straightforward life." I deadpanned that line, and Seamus made a small wolf snickering noise beside me.

Gwen smiled.

"Fine, maybe not *too many* fantasy books, but still. I'm not evil, I just need help. I would have asked you at the end of your 'quest' anyway, but I figured since I had you here, and you brought up the idea of owing me…"

"Fine," I put my hands up in a gesture of surrender. "I'll work for you. I certainly owe you after that last bit, and…well, whatever, I like the idea of helping people anyway."

In retrospect, I really should have asked more about the fine print.

"Great!" Gwen said.

And then a thousand lightning bolts struck me at once.

Or that's what it felt like, anyway. As though I were being ripped apart at the atomic level and rebuilt by lightning. I didn't even have time to scream.

When I could open my eyes again, I looked down at my body, expecting to find myself scrambled into a million microscopic pieces, or glowing, or… something. But I still looked normal, or as normal as a naked woman with a death grip on the fur of a wolf could look.

"Sorry, Seamus," I muttered, releasing his fur. I inspected my hands and arms, but found nothing different.

"You won't notice much… visibly different. And as to the rest… well, my powers affect everyone who takes them on differently, so… you'll just have to practice to find out what you can do."

"Well, that's vague."

Gwen glared at me.

"My power is vast and affects everyone differently. Imagine a list of all the things you *might* be able to do right now. Think of how fun it would be for the reader to go through all of that."

"Good point," I admitted. "Now, how about we go save Trevor and Sol."

Gwen nodded.

"You should be able to get yourselves there now. Just keep a good hold on anyone you need to bring with you and, if you can manage it, bring anyone injured back here."

That reminded me.

"My shoulder—"

ALL FIXED.

I guess Life was still paying attention to us.

"Oh. Cool. Thanks."

Sure enough, trying to move my shoulder and arm wasn't excruciating in any way.

IT HAS BEEN FIXED SINCE YOU ARRIVED AT THE CLEARING. SIMPLY BEING IN MY PRESENCE WILL HEAL ALL INJURIES.

"Well, that's useful," I muttered. And then I reached through space and time and pulled us back to Sol and Trevor.

UNFORTUNATELY, SOL AND Trevor were still fighting their way down the side of the cliff.

Luckily, Seamus shifted to human again as soon as we materialized on the cliff face. Oddly, we were both now wearing clothes. Huh. Something to wonder about, when I wasn't busy trying to rescue my friends and family from an onslaught of homicidally angry mages.

Since we'd somehow managed to pull ourselves to exactly where Sol seemed to be, and it appeared to be only seconds after we had been whisked away by Gwen, I suppose I shouldn't have been surprised that we also arrived facing the cliff wall, and in a position to grab hold of it without tumbling to our deaths. Apparently, reality was taking a break for a bit, as I wielded power that made even less sense than my ability to turn into a large, furry predator. Fun times.

Whatever, reality could suck it. I was going to use the hell out of this to save the people I cared about.

Seamus snarled, despite being in human form, as more spells were slung in our general direction, and he made his way toward Sol, while I started gesturing wildly to get Trev's attention.

Trev seemed busy leading the mages' spell-flinging attention on a bit of wild Phoenix chase, and it took me a good thirty seconds to signal to him that he needed to head my way.

When he finally turned and saw me, I thought he might fall out of the sky—his wings stopped moving for a full heartbeat. Luckily they were still extended outwards, rather than down.

I would love for you to torch these guys, but maybe we should just go, I sent to him, once I belatedly remembered that I could just think things at him instead of speaking or gesturing wildly.

I didn't know how much I could do with the new powers Gwen had given me, but the only thing I was *sure* I could do was the one thing that made the most sense anyway. It was time to get the hell out of Dodge.

YOU'RE ALIVE!

Trev managed to convey his levels of both surprise and elation at the news that I wasn't a fresh serving of human burger all along the valley floor, and I just barely managed to keep his concern and excitement from completely swamping me.

I will happily explain it all in a minute, once we're safe somewhere. For now, we just need to go.

Trevor nodded his flaming bird head, and shared a feeling of affirmation through our twin bond just in case he was too far away for me to see, which, when you added in all the fire and spells flying through the air, he was. He winged his way towards me, and I could see Seamus and Sol working their way closer along the cliff as well. I was certain that if I could touch everyone, or at least if we were all touching each other, I could get us all out of here and back to that forest. I just had to—

Fuck. A giant ball of... something nasty flew over my shoulder and left behind some rather disquieting blisters. Luckily, I still felt like I had most of my skin, and full control of my arm, unlike the last time a spell had grazed me that way. Soon, we weren't going to have much choice about how close we all got before I shifted away with whoever was touching me, and I didn't know if I'd get a chance for round two.

Trevor was almost within arm's reach (although I wasn't sure about how badly he'd burn me if I grabbed him) and Sol and Seamus were only one or two moves away from being within range when I heard the crack of rock breaking high above us. Someone had either wildly missed the mark with one of their spells, or they were simply trying to kill us with rockfall.

I didn't waste the moment it would take to curse the cowards who kept trying to kill us from the safety of the top of the cliff, but I promised myself I would take that moment later. Instead, I leapt for Seamus and Sol, covering the last few feet of distance between us and grabbing hold of each of them, screaming Trevor's name all the way.

I had to hope that Trevor would either dive for me, or just dive away from the wall. We didn't have time to hesitate before the refrigerator-sized chunk of cliff that was coming towards us was here and we were dead. We didn't have time for anything, actually. Only preternatural speed had gotten me to Sol and Seamus before the boulder got there. I willed us back to that circle of trees as hard as I could, and felt searing pain in my hip just before the world went black around us.

I CAME TO looking up at a starry sky through a
bunch of pine boughs. The air held the crisp
scent of autumn in the mountains; a mixture
of fallen leaves, pine needles, and cool wind. Considering the two mountainous regions I'd been
flashing between lately, that didn't really narrow
things down.

I sat up.

My body objected strenuously to the movement,
and made said objections known by forcibly eject-
ing everything I'd eaten in the past 24 hours.

I lay down again.

"Vic?"

The voice was weak, or maybe that was just my
hearing, but I recognized it.

"Trev?" I asked.

I vaguely recalled being worried about Trev earlier. He had been in decidedly mortal peril. "You alive?" I figured it wouldn't hurt to check. The afterlife might have stars and pine boughs too.

"Yep. You?"

I tried to nod, but when that small motion almost made me heave again, I settled on whispering a weak little, "yes," before lying completely still.

"What did you do?" Trev asked.

"Dunno." How little could I move and still vocalize my replies? "Gwen gave me some powers. Thought they might work to save our butts."

"I'd say you were right."

I smiled. That, at least, didn't make me feel sick.

"How long have I been out?"

Trev was quiet a moment.

"Only a couple of hours. I'm surprised it wasn't longer, actually, with all the healing you must have done."

That made me want to sit up, but I had learned my lesson. I took a very long time to bring my head up from the leafy ground on which it was pillowed.

"I didn't heal anyone," I said, once I was sure my stomach wasn't going to try escaping through my throat again. "The tree does that."

I looked around for Life. I didn't see the glowing eyes, but we did seem to be in the same clearing, with the tree shaped like a hooded figure carrying a scythe.

"I meant you. You needed a lot of healing."

"I did?"

I finally locked eyes on Trevor. He was sitting on the pine needle covered forest floor a few feet away from me, with his arms wrapped around his knees.

"I might have singed you a bit," he admitted quietly.

"That's ok, Trev." I took in his appearance. He was wearing a simple pair of jeans and a black t-shirt, sensible boots, and a stainless steel watch.

"Where'd you get your stuff?" I asked. As far as I could remember, we'd all been naked the last time we'd been in human form. Or had Seamus and I found clothes somehow? My memory was a bit hazy. "Did you shove your clothes in a dimensional pocket or something?"

He smiled at that.

"I do have a tendency to singe things, so that wouldn't be a bad idea. But I'm not actually sure why I'm dressed this way. We all materialized with clothes on, when we got to this clearing."

Well, that was interesting.

"Was I awake?" I asked.

He shook his head.

"Not in a way that counted, no."

"Hm… I was wondering if it was part of Gwen's power, but if it happened with me unconscious…"

"Gwen's power?"

"Yeah I… it's a long story. So, where are Seamus and Sol?" I asked, before I could get too sidetracked by the question of mystery outfits and meddling deities.

"They went to your place to clean up and make food. They said they'd meet us there. I didn't see any reason for them to stick around and watch you sleep, when I was here to keep an eye on things and light anyone suspicious on fire. They agreed, although the wolf pup howled about it."

That made me chuckle a bit. I didn't find Seamus' overprotective streak attractive or endearing, but it was kind of funny sometimes. He was nothing if not consistent.

"Were they ok?"

Trevor nodded.

"They were all healed up the second we arrived in the clearing. The only one who needed extra time was you."

That was odd. If anything, I would have thought that Gwen's powers would have made healing easier, rather than more time-consuming.

IT IS NOT PHYSICAL HEALING THAT HAS FORCED YOU TO REST.

"Oh hey, Life," I said.

Trevor was looking around the clearing a bit frantically. It looked like he was trying to find anything *other* than a talking tree to attribute that voice to, but he was, of course, failing.

"Trev, this is the Tree of Life. Life, this is my brother Trev."

A PLEASURE TO MEET YOU.

My introduction seemed to confirm Trevor's wildest fears, but at least he seemed to know where to look now.

"Umm… likewise? Thanks for the healing."

YOU ARE WELCOME. VIC, YOU MUST GO HOME. EAT HUMAN FOODS AND REST. YOU CONSUMED ALMOST ALL OF YOUR MAGIC. IF YOU DO NOT REST, YOU MAY INADVERTENTLY TAKE YOUR OWN LIFE.

"Well, that's not on my list of things to do. We'd better get going, Trev."

Honestly, it didn't take much to convince me that I should be at home. In addition to being where I could find both of my friends—was it sad that I could count all my friends on one hand at this stage?—it was a place where I could lie down for a few hours and safely munch on all the pizza I could possibly need to refuel my magic-weary body.

That was a weird idea—that I could be magic-weary—but I was too tired to deal with it at that moment.

Trevor stood up and I turned towards home. Weirdly, despite the fact that we were in the middle of a clearing in the woods that I had only been to twice before, I knew exactly which direction home was.

Just as my body began to protest the mere idea of walking home from here, Gwen popped into existence and grabbed us both.

~~~

I was both relieved and grateful to find that Gwen had taken us to my place rather than… anywhere else in the world. Honestly, with Gwen I never knew what to expect. I was pretty sure her intentions were good, but she and I often had different ideas of what constituted "helpful."

"Rest up for a while, Vic," she said, as she gingerly helped me to one of the stools around my kitchen island. "You're not used to channeling that kind of power, and it's pretty different from what it takes to call your snow leopard in through the dark matter running in your veins, so it'll take you a while to recover until you get used to it, and… well,
~~~

even then, you can still use too much and do your-self some serious damage."

My brain stuttered over so many parts of that explanation that I didn't even know where to start. Self preservation took over my mouth for me, though, and I asked, "How long until it's safe for me to use the power again?"

"Whenever you stop feeling like walking across the room is akin to climbing Everest, you're probably on the road to recovery. Honestly, just like with anything else in life, when you feel rested and whole you're good to go, and if you feel ragged and awful, you're not. There's no trick to it, outside of practice."

Well, that was both reassuring and not. Of course, it would have been sweet if my newfound powers were limitless and never strained me, but that would have been too much like some poorly considered fantasy gimmick, where the rules of magic mold to fit the author's purposes, and were only limited randomly, when it suited the plot. Even though Gwen had claimed to be my narrator, and then I had "taken over"… I didn't believe that I was in a book. Or if I was, it wasn't *that* kind of book. My life had never been that easy.

Whatever, I should be stoked that I could suddenly will myself through time and space. It didn't have to be easy. It was already ridiculous enough that I could turn myself into a snowleopard without much strain. Now, I had suddenly added Whovian style powers to my arsenal. I was all for it. Or I would be. As soon as I could have a nap.

I woke up sometime the next day blinking groggily at Cary Elwes & Robin Wright cutting their way through the fire swamp. It was nice to open my eyes in my own room, staring at one of my favorite posters, even if I was dismayed to find that I had passed out before I'd had a chance to interrogate Gwen. As I slowly stretched my way out of bed, and plodded to my shower, I was relieved to discover that my brain and muscles now moved slightly faster than molasses in January.

Gwen may have left, but Sol, Seamus, and Trev were all present when I made my way down to the kitchen, throwing on the least-dirty clothes piled on my floor.

"Vic!" everyone chorused, as I jumped the last couple steps and skidded into the kitchen/dining area.

They were all perched on stools around the kitchen island, noses buried in mugs of hot beverages, until their heads popped up collectively at my less than subtle entrance.

I waved and then bowed, because what else do you do when you walk into a room full of people happy to see you?

"Hey folks," I said, making a direct line to the half-full pot of coffee I spied on the kitchen counter next to the fridge. "Whichever of you dug out the pot and made coffee is my new hero."

Seamus raised a hand and waved it casually.

"About time I managed to rescue you, instead of the other way around," he said, smiling.

I poured coffee and scowled at him.

"You have done plenty to save my ass in the short time we've known each other. And saving me isn't a prerequisite to being my friend, or anything."

Now Seamus was raising both hands.

"Calm down, Vic. It was a joke. I'm perfectly happy with the number of times you've saved my ass."

I kept the glare going, just for appearance's sake.

"Somebody woke up grumpy," said Trev, waving his mug of green tea at me. I marveled at the fact that I could smell it from where I stood, still five feet away from him. This whole feline senses when not in a feline body thing was both interesting and weird.

"I'm grumpy," I said, as I walked over to join them all at the tile-topped kitchen island, "because I woke up with a thousand questions buzzing through my head, and my primary source of answers is off doing… Gwen knows what."

I chuckled internally at my word choice. Gwen certainly would know what she was doing. Unlike the rest of us.

"We might be able to piece together a bit for you," Sol said, her smile making my stomach tighten again. She was dressed now, and I wondered what she'd done for clothes, as the ones she was wearing didn't look like mine. I guess she'd had plenty of time to head out and buy stuff while I was sleeping. I filed it away as way too low on the priority list to ask about now, and instead listened as she continued talking.

"We've been trying to piece things together all morning."

"Is it even safe to talk here?" I asked.

Trev nodded. "I've taken care of any monitoring 'devices' that were left behind."

The way he said devices made me think that some of said devices might actually be spells.

"How far have you gotten in unravelling our mysteries, then?" I asked, looking around at all three of them.

My heart stuttered for a moment, as I realized how damned relieved I was to see them all here and in one piece. I didn't have many friends. I mean, I'd had a few friends in Colorado growing up, but most of them hadn't known how to act around me after my parents had died, and I had run off to Arizona before they'd had a chance to figure it out. They might be there for me in the future, they might not. But these three people… these three people were my rocks now. It hadn't taken long, fuck, if you considered the fact that I'd only known Trevor for eight years before he was taken from us, I hadn't known any of them as long as my friends in Colorado. And I'd only known Seamus and Sol for a handful of days… but I already knew I could count on them. I knew that if someone was trying to kill me, they'd try to stop them. That they would risk their own lives to save mine, and that I would do the same for them. I'm not sure there was a higher bar for friendship, and I certainly didn't want to find out if there was. I took a deep breath, blinked until the tears that had threatened to do more than make my vision fuzzy disappeared, and then focused on what Sol was saying.

"Well, luckily, Seamus was around when you got turned all Agent-of-Gwen, so he was able to explain how the hell you managed to flit in and out of nowhere to save our butts back on the cliff."

I nodded, appreciating not having to go through that part again.

"Though," Sol continued, "he never did explain how you managed to find time to get dressed while Gwen had you whisked away to that clearing."

I quirked my eyebrows for a second, unsure what she was talking about, and then remembered that Seamus and I had both appeared fully clothed when we returned to the cliff.

"Probably the same way that all four of us were fully dressed when we materialized in the clearing yesterday," Trevor suggested.

I hadn't been conscious for that part, but I had noticed that Trev and I were indeed both fully clothed when I came to. After thinking about it for a minute, something occurred to me. That first time I'd met Gwen, she'd been naked at first and then had conjured clothes out of nowhere, magically converting them into an entirely different outfit later.

"Gwen's power certainly lets her shift clothing around however she likes. Maybe it's part of my new arsenal of magic."

That had eyebrows raised all around.

"What's the big deal, guys? Wardrobe change is hardly something noteworthy on the list of badass talents a person can have."

They all chuckled.

"You clearly haven't been a werecat very long," Trev said, still smiling.

"Well, duh." I said.

"The rest of us have had longer to get frustrated with always having to carry clothes in our mouths, or stash them somewhere convenient, or just get used to being naked in front of people, which is fine for us, but generally weirds out norms."

"You mean nons?" I asked.

"He means muggles," Sol said, smirking. "And he's right, many of us would trade a limb for the convenience of not having to deal with the clothing fiasco in the modern world."

I just stared at all three of them.

"A limb?"

Sol just shrugged. "Ok, maybe not a limb. After all, sometimes it's nice to just be naked whenever you feel like it, which is certainly how we handle things in a community of weres, but…"

"But it's a pain in the ass if you're surrounded by mages," Trev grumbled. "They're superior gits at the best of times, and add in the necessity of going naked to use your were powers, and you have to burn the crap out of quite a few of them just to keep them from teasing you every time you shift."

That made me laugh.

"Ok, so clearly you three will just have to stick with me forever, so I can always conjure clothes for you. Next item?"

"How about the reports I got from my supervisor last night about a fire-drake wiping out most of MOME's Bolivian facility?" Sol asked.

"Wait. What?!" Seamus and I asked, in unison.

Trev just smirked a bit, leading me to believe that he knew something about that.

"Apparently," Sol continued, "after we escaped MOME, a few fire demons and some selkies wreaked havoc in the lower levels, causing a massive evacuation of MOME, which, combined with a massive security breach disarming most of the wards in and around the building, caused all the people being held by MOME to be released."

"Well, that was the plan wasn't it?" I asked. "Didn't we mean to release all of the kids that MOME had taken over the years?"

Sol glared daggers at Trevor.

"We were supposed to be releasing the children, but *everyone* MOME was holding escaped. Some of whom may very well have deserved to be held."

I looked at Trev, wondering what his reply would be. He simply shrugged.

"We didn't have time to be choosy about who was released, and besides, who died and made us the arbiters of all justice? Who am I to judge who deserved to be in MOME's clutches and who didn't? MOME is a dishonest organization from the core. I can't be sure that their reasons for holding anyone are legitimate, so it just made sense to let everyone go."

"But what about the serious criminals?" Seamus asked.

"How could we have determined who those were in any reasonable amount of time? Not to mention figuring out how to release everyone else but them? Besides, it sounds like being caught in the facilities yesterday would have been a death sentence. Did they all deserve to die?"

That left both Sol and Seamus quiet, and I had to admit that I didn't have any answers to Trev's questions. I had a hard time believing that MOME's idea of justice was in any way unbiased, so how could we possibly have discerned who deserved freedom and who didn't, even if we'd had enough time, which we certainly hadn't?

"Ok. Can we get back to this fire-drake business?" I asked, trying to contain my excitement.

"Was there seriously a dragon there? Am I misunderstanding fire-drake? What happened?!"

Sol sighed.

"The report I read said that after the building had been evacuated, a large, black-scaled fire-drake began immolating the entire premises."

Trev's smile was so wide that I had a hard time not laughing.

"You know exactly who that was, don't you?" I asked.

He shrugged and I punched his shoulder playfully.

"Ow. Hey! What was that for? You know just as well as I do who it was."

I just stared at him for a minute, until a memory came back to me. A sibilant voice in the darkness. A beautiful young woman with iridescent ebony skin and reptilian irises…

"No way!" I said, punching Trev's shoulder again.

"Seriously, Vic. Ow. Stop punching me. You're a lot stronger than you used to be."

I stared at him, baffled. He'd never used to whine about our sibling arm punches when we were kids, but ok, fine. He certainly didn't have to let me punch him. Honestly, it was a habit I thought I'd grown out of after I'd started actually training in martial arts, but apparently something about having my brother back made me jump back in time to when we'd still spent every day together.

"Sorry, Trev," I said, wrapping him in a hug instead. "So, you want to tell us how you know Rhelia?"

"We're friends," he shrugged, pushing me off of him.

I do not want to talk about this now, he added, just to me.

I sighed.

"Fine," I said. "Be all mysterious about it. What about the kids? And what about Rhelia? Did she escape? Have you heard from any of them? Did MOME not manage to round everyone up again after they took care of the fire?"

Trev chuckled briefly.

"There was no 'taking care' of that fire, Vic. And yes, I put Rhelia in charge of getting the kids to safety, so I'm sure they all got somewhere where MOME will have a very hard time tracking them."

"Well that's a relief," I said, and looked at Sol and Seamus, who also looked satisfied with that response, at least.

Then a thought struck me.

"Wait a second. Is Rhelia… your girlfriend?" I asked. "Is she the main reason we went back there?"

My jaw dropped at the thought that Trev could be romantically involved with a woman as… intimidating as Rhelia had seemed. Not because that would be a bad thing, just because… well, Trev was pretty laid back, and Rhelia seemed pretty no-nonsense to me.

I said I don't want to talk about it, Trev complained mentally.

"Whatever," I hastily added, waving the topic away as if it horrified me—which it absolutely did not—before Sol or Seamus could ask any follow-up questions. "I want to talk about the paperwork I tracked down in MOME, anyway. We still need to look at that together."

"Wait," Sol said, not allowing me the change in topic I was hoping for, "you both know the firedrake?"

A sharp knock on the door conveniently made it so that neither Trev nor I had to reply.

I looked at Trevor, who closed his eyes for a moment, then nodded.

"Uncle Algernon," he said, his eyebrows rising. "Why on earth is he here?"

"What day is it?" I asked. I'd left my phone upstairs after my shower.

"The 21st," said Seamus.

I nodded.

"It's the day he usually checks in with me," I said, getting up to go to the door. "And you're going to have to explain how you just checked my front porch from the kitchen table without a device, Trev."

When I opened the door, I found uncle Algernon, which I had expected, thanks to Trevor's warning. And a gun pointed right at my chest, which I had not.

Vic's adventures continue in *Victoria Marmot and the Inconvenient Prophecy*, and *Victoria Marmot and the Shadow of Death* (out now)!

Victoria Marmot Books 4, 5, and 6 are coming soon!

The Chronicles of Gensokai Series:
Blade's Edge
Traitor's Hope

Short stories:
Rain on a Summer's Afternoon

Follow Virginia on social media:
www.virginiamcclain.com
twitter.com/gwendamned
facebook.com/virginiamcclainauthor

ACKNOWLEDGEMENTS

These books wouldn't have been possible without a fair bit of help from a number of people. My deepest gratitude goes out to the following people:

My editor, Aurora Wilson-McClain, for not only working with my sometimes ridiculous deadlines, but also for helping me sort out the best use of obscure spell references, the number of "s"s a certain dragon uses in her speech patterns, and where, exactly, everyone has left their clothes.

My husband, for putting up with me disappearing every evening for months on end in order to get these books written, for being my best cheerleader and for not giving me too much grief when I failed to get my half of the housework done.

Cedar, for letting me ignore her often enough to get formatting done, as well as promotion and marketing stuff, and for being so willing to hang out with her wonderful caregivers.

Anne, Lee, Jim, and Gabi, for keeping Cedar entertained, fed, and happy so that I could write.

To my Patreon supporters: Paul, Corey, Mishy, and Jessica.

And finally, the folks at Stella's au CCFM for always putting up with me occupying a table for hours on end while only ordering a cup of tea.

Virginia McClain is an author who masqueraded as a language teacher for a decade or so. When she's not reading or writing she can generally be found playing outside with her four legged adventure buddy and the tiny human she helped to build from scratch. She enjoys climbing to the tops of tall rocks, running through deserts, mountains, and woodlands, and carrying a foldable home on her back whenever she gets a chance. She's also fond of word games, and writing descriptions of herself that are needlessly vague.

For more information check out
www.virginiamcclain.com
facebook.com/virginiamcclainauthor
twitter.com/gwendamned
bookbub.com/author/virginia-mcclain